WRATH

THE CHARITY DEACON INVESTIGATIONS
BOOK 7

P A WILSON

Ebook ISBN: 978-1-990509-19-3
Paperback ISBN: 978-1-990509-20-9
Audio book ISBN:978-1-990509-21-6

FREE EBOOK

Claim your copy of Buying Into Death when you use the QR code to sign up for my newsletter and follow Charity as she solves her fastest case yet!

1

W e'd been at it for an hour, and I was already sick to the eyebrows of hearing about the rules. David and I were in Andy's office, in a nondescript building a few blocks from the police station. The building designers hadn't planned on an office being jammed in a corner unless it was some design feature to put a concrete support post smack in the middle.

"We don't just jump in and sort out the details later, Charity." Andy pushed his chair back, bumping the windowsill.

"I understand, really. You need to do it a certain way, so the charges stand up in court. I just didn't think you expected me to investigate the same way." My entire business was built on getting the evidence and sorting out the paperwork later. It worked when you only had to satisfy the client. "If you won't give me any leeway, I'm no use."

David touched my arm to get my attention. And I realized I was halfway to standing in my frustration.

"You will have some," he said. "Just not full freedom. Because of the other reason we don't work like you do."

I looked at him, hoping for more.

"Because people die. We aren't investigating someone embezzling from payroll. Our targets fight back."

Mine did too, often enough. They didn't usually carry guns, though. "I get that. You were seconded to the RCMP. Are their rules the same as the VPD? I worked well with them."

He actually rolled his eyes. I couldn't argue. My definition of working well was different from his.

"We caught the killer," I said, trying to ignore the touch of teenage angst in my voice.

Andy stood and faced the window. It had a view of the side of the building next door — gray brick and no windows looking back. It didn't hold his attention for more than a few seconds. He turned back, looking calmer, and sat.

"Let's start again." He waited for me to nod. "Okay, Detective Anchor, you read the requirements for your secondment?"

David nodded. "And I understand the role of liaison with the civilian consultant." That was me.

"Ms. Deacon, you still have questions I'm not sure we can answer, but I'll try."

The formality kind of worked. It reminded me I was in RCMP territory, and not because I'm a pain in the ass. I was a valuable resource — they'd invited me, after all, and not just to keep an eye on me.

"Okay. I think it comes down to why I'm part of the team." I put aside the last hour of trying to work this exact question out and summarized. "I know we can't define it specifically, but you want me for the exact reason you are having difficulty answering my questions. I work alone most of the time. I improvise. I don't plan ahead much. I get results."

"Yes." Andy didn't try to clarify.

"So, off the record, we agree that if I feel the need to go and do my own thing, you won't try to stop me. You won't automatically try to protect me when things get risky. You'll listen when I suggest something a little outside your regulations."

Andy looked at David. Hoping he'd talk me into being sensible?

"As a cop," David said, "I will allow you to use the skills we hired you for. As your... boyfriend? I can't promise not to save your life if I think it needs doing."

Boyfriend. We needed a better word for that because people in their thirties didn't have boyfriends, and partner was too cold. Lover? Well, just let me groan at that.

I turned to Andy. Our relationship was purely professional. Maybe we'd move up to friendship level, but not yet — maybe never.

He sighed. "We did bring you on for your ability to accomplish things. Will you listen to me when I say you are endangering the case?"

It couldn't hurt to promise I'd listen. No one was talking about obeying yet. "I will. So, can we get to the part where we decide what to do?"

A long enough pause that I thought one of them would try to rein me in.

"I think Viktor McCarthy is our best bet to start with," Andy said. "He's got to be worried, because the rest of the child trafficking team is dead or in custody. Turning him might lead us to Ivan Kuznetsov, which is our goal. No matter what we're investigating at the moment, Kuznetsov is our target."

Viktor and his wife ran the private adoption agency supplied with kids who were bought by Ivan's organization. The ones they didn't use for slavery or prostitution, that is.

"You know where he is?"

Andy pulled a file from his desk drawer. "We're following some leads, but he's in hiding. If Kuznetsov finds out first, we'll be picking up a corpse if we're lucky."

"What about his wife?" I couldn't let them forget about the collateral. Cynthia might or might not be a good contact. My gut was telling me she instigated the connection with the Russian gang. But I had nothing to point to for proof.

"Can't find any clues," David said. "She might be with Viktor or gone to ground somewhere else."

"Or maybe Ivan has her hunting for him too," I said. "Did you find anything on her background?"

Andy flipped a page. "She's changed her name so many times, it's taking forever to build the profile. So far, we think she escaped from Chechnya just after Russia took back control. She could be a refugee from the violence, or a KGB agent, or the daughter of an Oligarch. We keep looking and finding new stories."

I moved her down my mental list of possible informants. "So, my first job is finding Viktor McCarthy?"

"You have some interesting sources," Andy said. "I'm not saying ours are squeaky clean — they wouldn't be any help if they were — but you seem to get more answers than we do from the same... institutions."

Nice way of referring to the Hells Angels. Andy had a point. When I got information, it wouldn't result in a raid on the gang headquarters. So, less filter on the details.

"I'll see what I can do."

Getting hold of Guy was always an adventure in stalking. He didn't always reply to my texts or calls. We had to balance his real fear that the gang would retaliate if they knew he was passing on information with his feeling of obligation to me for keeping his nephew on the straight path. The kid didn't need any more guidance from me, but Guy still figured he owed me. And I tried not to ask questions about the gang's activities. Being in that world gave Guy information on all kinds of criminal activity.

Today he did respond to my text. *Stay away from me.*

I responded with a grinning emoji.

The last time we spoke, he was protecting me from his gang-mate, Stick, by telling him I was his junkie, stalker, disease-riddled ex-girlfriend. That was unlikely to work another time. And I couldn't ask Andy or David to track his phone because I didn't want to lose Guy as an informant.

He was so hard to find the last time, I'd made a change. When I had to hang out in a filthy alley in the Downtown Eastside, I put a not-so-legal 'find my phone' tracker on his number. If he found out, he'd change his phone and I wouldn't get the new digits. I couldn't think of any reason he might find out.

The app showed his location at the bar nearest the Hells Angels house. Of course, the downside of that was I had no idea if he was drinking alone, with the entire chapter, or with his sister and the kids. At this time in the morning, I'd put money on it being the gang.

It took me a half hour to get to the pub. Long enough for Guy to have moved on, so I checked the app. Still there. I parked in the lot, facing the exit, just in case our friend Stick was with Guy and feeling frisky.

Inside the lighting was dim, probably to hide the stains on the carpet, and some of the damage to the chairs and tables. It wasn't doing a great job. Guy sat with two other Angels, neither of them Stick. I took a stool at the bar, so he'd see me eventually, and ordered a beer which I had no intention of drinking.

There was a cracked mirror behind the bar that let me keep an eye on the table. It took about ten minutes for Guy to end his chat and head up to order a new drink. The other two guys sauntered out the back door and we were as alone as we could be in a room half full of day drinkers.

"Death wish?" Guy asked.

I pushed my beer to him and laughed.

"What do you want this time, Charity?" He drank down half the pint in one go. I hoped he didn't plan on riding his bike anytime soon.

"If you don't want to be my source, just tell me." We'd had this conversation a couple of times now.

"Okay. Thanks for the beer." He finished it and put the glass down. He didn't walk away.

"I'm looking for Viktor McCarthy."

"Didn't taking down that Blackhouse guy and the Guptas finish the case?" He signaled for the bartender to pour another beer.

"You are walking, right?" I asked. "I'm not going to hear about a tragic death from mixing beer with a Harley."

"Took a cab. Got work to do here all day. Why?"

If he didn't know anything, Guy would have sent me away by now. "There's more than just the Blackhouse case to consider," I said. "Viktor and his wife could set up again with another team. I'm sure his boss won't want to lose the revenue stream." No need to mention Kuznetsov yet.

He turned to me and then glanced around. No one was paying attention. The barman was talking to the waitress while he filled glasses.

"Tell me you aren't going up against Ivan Kuznetsov alone."

Technically, I could answer truthfully. "He's too big and dangerous for anyone to take down alone."

"I don't know where McCarthy went to ground. I hear he's still in town, and you're right; he's setting up again. There aren't a lot of choices for a guy like that."

"Kuznetsov hasn't killed him yet?" It was a big possibility that we hadn't found the body yet — or ever would.

"No. He blamed the mess on Blackhouse. If he gets to him, then that might change."

"Alan Blackhouse is protected," I said. He'd taken a deal and was busy telling the authorities the little he knew about the Russian mob. "What exactly have you heard about McCarthy?"

"He's not going back into the paid adoption racket. He's found another angle into the people trafficking business. I have no idea what it is or where he is."

The Angels kept their sex trafficking to running adults,

not kids. If I could get their chapter boss to talk, I would probably get more, but I don't have a burning desire to be killed. And I wouldn't push Guy to find out more than was healthy for him. Dead contacts were useless, and I kind of liked him for protecting his nephew — and me a lot of the time. "Is it kids?" I asked just to be sure nothing major had changed.

"There's a lot of heat on that right now, thanks to you. So, probably not."

"Isn't he cutting into your business if he's going into adults?"

"Fuck, Charity. You can't have it both ways. I'm your contact, and I can't help you without doing what I'm supposed to do. The Angels don't keep members who don't get their hands dirty."

I didn't need reminding of that. All PIs used sources on the dark side of the street. "I meant, would your boss shut him down?"

Guy thought for a minute. I hoped it wasn't about whether or not he should walk away from me. Then he finished his beer and turned to me. "There's plenty of room for new players in that field. And if Kuznetsov wants to take our business, I'm not sure we can stop him. Look for McCarthy around the docks. That's how people sneak in here when they don't have papers."

He walked toward the restrooms before I could ask anything else.

3

G oing to the docks was a good idea. I had a few contacts who'd usually talk about shady things with me, but I had no idea if they were on shift. And the area was too big to just wander around, as it was mostly filled with stacked containers as far as the eye could see.

I wouldn't know if the lead was good unless I went, so I headed west. It would take almost an hour.

David called as I merged onto the highway.

"Where are you?"

"Hello to you, too. So nice to hear your voice."

"It's always a treat to talk to you, Charity. Do you have any leads?"

Man, I'm gone for not quite an hour, and he's worried I've blown the case? "Not much of one." I gave him the details — at least the important one, that my next destination was Delta Port.

"Can I help?"

Bringing a cop would stop my contacts from talking to

me. Although, bringing a cop would also open up new official avenues. And I was supposed to be playing on a team. No matter how much I hated the idea, I shouldn't go solo without a reason.

"Maybe. What do you think I need help with?"

"I can get you access. The VPD is one of the agencies policing the port, so maybe I've got an in. I can access the RCMP as well since I'm seconded. I have a friend in the Border Services too."

Access was easier than David thought. I didn't think it was a good idea to explain that to him — he might make a report that closed doors I wanted kept open. The questions running around my mind sounded a bit like a job interview. "I'm not sure official sources are a good way to find out if someone is hanging around trying to set up a people trafficking business. What else have you got to offer me?"

He chuckled. "A couple of sources in the grayer areas. You think Viktor is hanging out looking to steal someone's shipment?"

I couldn't see that happening, but how else was he going to start up? "Stealing a shipment of people would be too risky. But making contacts? Middleman, right? The kids arrived and he got names to pass on?"

"Yeah, the Guptas handled the supply. Crap, I hate talking about people like they are widgets."

If I thought of them as people, I just got mad. It tore at me to think what Nora went through before Glenda adopted her. I had the feeling I would learn how bad it could get through this investigation.

"Why don't you introduce me to your contact," I said. The real problem was having my sources see me with David, a cop. Like Guy, I guess they'd heard we were together, but that's very different from bringing a cop into a relationship based on secrets and trust.

"Or you could introduce me to yours."

"No, I think I'll hold back on revealing my sources. I guess we need to meet somewhere." I couldn't think of a place close to the entrance. Delta Port stuck out into the Pacific off the highway, with no convenient shopping mall or Starbucks.

"Are you on the 17?"

It was the best way to get from Coquitlam to Delta, but he didn't know where I'd started. Or he shouldn't. "Yes."

"Meet me in Tsawwassen Mills. The food court? I missed lunch."

I'd forgotten the mall was close to the exit for the port. That area seemed like just a blob of land to me. Somewhere ferries came and went, a mall, and a nice little suburb. My stomach growled at the idea of a greasy slice of pizza. "I can meet you in about fifteen minutes. That work?"

"Yep. We should take one car in. I could drop you off before I head to the office and my official sources."

It would be helpful to get access, but I would be stuck on his schedule. "We can talk about it over lunch."

He ended the call, and I flicked on the radio. Normally I listen to podcasts or my own playlist, but today I needed the news.

By the time I parked the car and headed to the mall, I knew the weather forecast, the latest hockey gossip, and more than enough about political maneuvering from across the border. I needed bad-for-me food and a large soda. Maybe a little shopping when I finished my research.

Like most retail outlets, the food court sat in the middle of a maze of stores. The map makes it look like a straight line from an entrance to the one place you want to be, but that's not what it felt like. Too many people wandering the walkways. Too many sales signs.

David was sitting at a table waiting for me. He stood as soon as he caught my eye and grinned like an idiot. Got to love a man who lights up for you.

4

W e took separate cars after deciding on our strategy. David would head to the office and try to find out if there were any anomalies. I would head over to where the workers gathered to grab gossip. I didn't argue much when he suggested the plan because it was what I wanted. David would just be in my way with the workers, and I'd be bored in the office.

I texted my contact to find out where he would meet me. The terminal wasn't the best place to be wandering around. Semis moved constantly to be hitched to a container-laden trailer. Pedestrians kept to the marked walkways. It's for their safety officially, but I'd always suspected that the people who designed the port were more interested in keeping traffic moving.

Zack, my contact, worked on bar code duty, meaning he stood in one high-traffic area and scanned a code on the paperwork for each driver as they headed out. At least it wasn't in the coal terminal today. Dirty, and a long walk to find him.

Taking a smoke break in five. Meet me in the usual place.

The usual place was off to the side of the traffic, facing the water. A few picnic tables sat in a row for the guys to eat and smoke. I say guys, but there were almost as many female workers directing trucks as male.

It was a nice day for sitting in the open, not too hot and not raining. Delta Port sat out in the ocean unlike the smaller ports downtown. The breezes off the water cleared the exhaust enough to be able to smell the saltwater and a little hint of the coal piles farther along. Maybe my luck with the weather would extend to getting all the information I needed to grab Viktor McCarthy.

"Been a while," Zack said as he plunked himself on the bench beside me. In a crowd, he'd blend in. Face deeply tanned, hair bleached and thinning, he stood about five-ten and his body could best be described as medium scrawny. "I heard you were working with the feds."

He pulled out a pack of cigarettes, offered me one out of habit and lit up when I shook my head.

"I'm consulting. It's a job."

"No problem. You do your thing. I just meant I don't want them to know who I am."

He'd never given me anything but gossip. "Why? Aren't most of the people here informing to someone or other? Cops, reporters, criminals?"

Zack gave a chuckle that ended in a cough. "And all of us think the others are ratting on everyone. Or trying to horn in on the deal."

I guess if I worked in an industry with a reputation of things 'falling off a truck,' I'd be leery of people talking to the authorities. "I'll keep them away from you, don't worry."

"We'll see," Zack said. "What do you want today?"

"I'm looking for this guy." I showed him the picture of Viktor on my phone. "Seen him?"

"Maybe. What's in it for me?" He sucked in a drag that burned half the cigarette in one go.

Zack and I had a purely cash relationship. I didn't want to owe him a favor of any kind. "Two hundred? If it pans out."

"What's he done?" Zack lit a second cigarette from the stub of the first.

"You heard about the bust of that kid trafficking operation?" When he nodded, I continued, "I helped with it. This guy got away. I think he's going to try to set up again. Looking for a source to import people."

"Fucking assholes." Zack took another long drag while he decided what to tell me. I kept silent until he was ready. "If I knew who was helping the people traffickers, I'd tell you for free to shut them down."

"I believe you."

"We all know it's happening, but there's a small group of assholes who take care of it. They're told the containers to divert. They know the drivers, and most of them are doing it under threat."

"That's how it keeps going," I said. "I busted only a small part of the organization. But this guy slipped away. We think the mob boss is letting him set up again. If he fails this time, he's dead."

"And you aren't willing to let him fail?"

"There's no guarantee he would. Do you have anything for me?"

"I don't know who exactly. I don't know when either. You'll need your pals in blue to help you with it."

Did he want me to promise again not to involve him

with the cops? Or was he warning me to be careful? Why did they always do that? Zack was usually cool about handing over information without warning me off. Not like Guy, who prefaced everything these days with 'don't do it.'

"I'll take all the help I can get." I pulled out the cash. "What do you have?"

He looked around before putting the money in his pocket. "It might be nothing, understand? I like to keep informed, and sometimes I go nosing in where people don't expect me."

I hope he didn't plan to go looking for information for me. Digging into secrets about these guys would never be anything but crazy risky. "And?"

"Your man came here the other day. I saw him talking to one of the guys who usually works night shift."

So, Viktor was still alive.

"They were talking about a delivery. Your guy was asking about maybe getting a percentage of the cargo. If you think he's setting up, then he meant getting some of the people in the container. Telling the owner that they died."

Starting small and testing the supply chain. "Did he get them?"

"No. I'm not telling you who he was talking to, right? But let's call him Bill. Bill says he has no way to take a few. The container is sealed until it gets to the next stop. That your guy needs to talk to whoever opens it up."

"Did you get a name? Or a location?"

Zack looked over my shoulder and then stood. "I'm not giving you names, but you should look around Derwent and Chester. They unload in a warehouse there. Your guy might be hanging around tonight." Zack stubbed out his cigarette and headed back to his post, and I sat on the bench alone.

My phone buzzed; David. *Where are you?*

I replied that I was on my way back. I'd find out what he'd dug up before I shared Zack's lead. But I wasn't going to Annacis Island by myself when I had my own personal bodyguard boyfriend. One who had a gun and the ability to arrest anyone we found.

5

W e met at his car. No one was loitering, and mine was only a few spaces away. A good enough place to update the information.

"Are you keeping Andy informed?" I asked. I'm not sure why that suddenly popped into my head as the most important question. I didn't want the RCMP to show up because we dropped out of communication for a while, I guess. But they were good backup, and I wanted cruisers rolling to our aid if we needed them.

"Not every minute," David said. "He knows I'm here because he had a few names to give me. If we go after a lead, I'll let him know. I'm supposed to update him every day regardless. Is that okay with you, ma'am?"

I punched him in the arm for the sarcasm. "I guess it's better than relying on me to do it."

"We won't always be together, Charity. You need to touch base with him too."

After I promised not to go rogue, David pulled out a notebook and started giving me what he'd learned. "No sudden shift changes. No complaints about malingering.

Occasionally I get asked to fix a problem in exchange for information. A couple of last-minute delays in pick up, but nothing suspicious. Sorry, not much help."

He knew as well as I did that nothing being out of the ordinary was often as useful as a load of clear evidence at this point. "I got something we can maybe use," I said, trying not to sound like I didn't want to share.

He waited, I guess realizing it was hard for me to share a case, even when I'd agreed to it. I pushed aside the reluctance and added, "I can't tell you who. Please don't go looking, I need my contacts, and I'm not sure he'll be safe if you get involved."

"I could check the cameras, but I promise not to," David said.

The amount of crime that went on under the eye of the cameras boggled my mind. I told him what Zack gave me. "We should head to Annacis now," I said. "It'll be late enough for us to set up by the time we make it through the traffic."

David looked out across the cars parked around us. I followed his gaze. Nothing new since we got here. He was thinking, and I wasn't sure I wanted to hear the result.

"We are going," I said. "Both of us."

He nodded but didn't look back at me for long enough that I was about to start arguing my position when he finally spoke. "Yes, we are together on this. When we get there, that might change."

"No. I'm part of the team." I bit back the rest of the words boiling in my head. Not the time to fight back, but no way was he going to sideline me for my safety.

"You can't arrest anyone. Think about it. If we find McCarthy, you can't do anything but try to hold him until I can arrest him. So, you don't go all maverick, right?"

Unfortunately, the ability to arrest someone came with all kinds of rules and regulations. I didn't want any of it. "Of course not. But I am not sitting in the car while you do the work."

"Not what I planned. I think we should park somewhere safe and go in my car. I have tools that will let us find the right place."

I nodded for him to continue. Being in one car would make it easier to stay together. And he didn't need to know I had distance listening devices in my car.

"We find the right place. Either we see McCarthy, or we figure out the right place by process of elimination. Then we wait until we catch him."

That was way too passive for me. "If we've missed him, that won't work. I think we go inside and search the place when we figure out exactly where it is." I pulled out my phone and checked the location. "There are only three warehouses at that intersection. One of them is pretty separate from the others."

"Charity, I need a warrant."

I grinned at him. "See? I bring value. I don't need one."

"You are acting as an agent for the RCMP. That means you can't just break in and search."

Well, that takes away a lot of my value to the investigation. "I won't break in, I guess. I can wander in if it's open, and then call you if I need help. You come running in on exigent circumstances."

He pulled me in for a kiss. "I like your thinking, but let's wait until we arrive."

I'D BEEN RIGHT about the warehouse. David and I parked at McDonald's and took his car the short distance to Derwent and Chester. Two of the three warehouses belonged to national stores with brand name trucks parked in the bay. The other one looked deserted but not abandoned. No business name anywhere on the building. No cameras for security.

"So, we have no way of wandering in to chat with a worker or two." I was itching to use my picks on the padlock, but David's warning stopped me. I didn't want Viktor McCarthy to skip free on a technicality. And I could always come back later, alone.

"If we force our way in, it will tip off the gang and they'll move. Knowing about the location is valuable. We can set surveillance and catch a lot of bad guys." He pulled out his phone.

"Wait. I can go in and look around without leaving a trace. If I don't find anything, no loss. If I do, you can go in the right way."

David called a number from his contacts. I didn't see the name.

"I need a warrant to take a look inside a warehouse we suspect of being a stop on a people trafficking route," he said to whoever answered.

Good idea if we got it. But I could still sneak in to check if there was anything worthwhile before he got his answer.

"Thanks. I'll be here." He ended the call. "Five minutes. I need something from the trunk."

He came back with a parabolic listening device that was a better model than mine. "We can check if anyone is inside while we wait."

We needed to be closer than the car to catch anything, so we headed for a storage facility between our target and the car. David pointed it at a window in the door to the side of the bay. Nothing.

His phone vibrated. "Got it. No one is talking in there. Let's go."

I pulled out my picks and had the padlock open in thirty seconds. We opened the door enough to slip in and then closed it. The only light inside came from two dusty windows high in the back wall, but it was enough to show a few tire tracks, and mud confirmed a semi's presence not long ago.

"We're too late," I said.

David started walking the perimeter of the space. "Maybe something will be here. You go the other way, and we'll meet at the back."

In the far corner, I found a child's shoe and a pile of empty water bottles. Not quite enough proof that kids were transported here. I kept walking the wall, scanning the floor and walls until I met David. He was crouched down checking something on the floor, holding his phone to film whatever it was.

He ended the recording and stood. "Blood on the wall, lots. Some red hairs. And this." He pointed to a watch with a smashed face.

I pulled up the various pictures of Viktor I kept on my phone. "The watch is his," I said, showing the image to David.

"Our friend Viktor is in need of medical help."

6

"Where to next?" I knew what I would be doing if this was my case, but the cops must have a better way to find an injured suspect than scouring the area for clinics.

"The phone," David said. "We need to stay here until the crime scene team arrives, and they'll take elimination samples from us."

"When will that be?" Standing around watching David make calls didn't feel like an exciting evening. Maybe I could go looking for that shady clinic after all.

He made a call before answering me. "Not long. Stay here. I'll go get my car and we can at least sit in comfort while I find Viktor's doctor."

Unfortunately, his car was only across the street. No time for me to go in for another snoop or reach out to my contacts in secret to find the local doctor to the criminals. He jogged across and was back in the parking lot within a minute. I was able to send one text to Guy while I waited. He didn't respond immediately.

Inside the car was better than leaning against the side of the building.

"We've got about thirty minutes," David said as he pulled out his phone. "That blood wasn't dry, so maybe McCarthy is still being fixed up somewhere."

"If we can find him." It was a lot of blood, but that didn't mean life-threatening damage. Minor head wound, bloodied nose, both would have spurted. The hairs embedded into it didn't bode well though. "What if he didn't look for help?"

David was scrolling through a list of contacts. "Then we find him another way. Unless he was taken away and killed somewhere else, that's not enough blood loss to cause death. The closest vet is across the bridge in New West. There's a clinic in Surrey we suspect of doing unreported work for cash."

I checked my phone for a reply from Guy. Nothing yet. I took it off silent mode since we weren't sneaking up on anyone. I wanted to hear the tone if he reached out.

"Do you think he'll go to someone with ties to Kuznetsov? That sounds dangerous and stupid." If I were in Viktor's shoes, I would go find a doctor at his home. In fact, I would have set up my own doctors and lawyers just on the off chance I needed someone unconnected to the vicious crime boss I worked for. "Any family who might help him?"

"It's a good idea. Cynthia was an EMT at some point. But we can't find her either." He didn't look up from his screen. "I can find out if any 911 calls came in from around here. Cynthia would have friends who'd do her a favor, right?"

I looked at the vet and clinic sites. Nothing unsavory, but sewing up bullet wounds wasn't likely to be listed as a service. Although, the clinic did list day surgeries, so they had the equipment.

"Three calls out," David said. "Only one for a beating victim."

There was no odor of recently fired gun in the warehouse, so beating or stabbing. Where the blood hit the wall seemed to be right for a beating. A knife wound that spurted that high on the wall would have left a body. "Red haired tall guy?"

He chuckled. "They are getting the details; it'll take a bit."

Now, we waited. For the crime scene team, for a response from Guy, for information on the 911 call, and for the freedom to go looking at two possible places where a criminal could get help. That's when I put two and two together to find out we'd missed the obvious.

"If he's just beaten, he doesn't need to avoid the hospital emergency entrances. No one is compelled to report a beating, right? They might not even ask what happened, beyond a check for symptoms."

"Crap, yes. Okay, the closest hospitals are Royal Columbian or Surrey Memorial." David had them up on Google. He hit the number for Royal Columbian, and I held my breath.

The crime scene van drove up and parked next to us while David worked his way through the phone menu and a nosy receptionist. I got out and told them what we found inside and asked if they'd take our samples fast so we could leave.

By the time I got back in the car, David was talking to someone in the ER.

"Yes, he's our guy. Can you stall so we can take him in? No, I doubt he'll cause problems, but have security nearby. Yes, we'll be no more than fifteen minutes." Then he laughed and ended the call.

"You got a lot of information without some kind of warrant."

"A buddy. He said McCarthy has been waiting half an hour, another fifteen minutes won't scare him off."

A tech knocked on the window with a pack of swabs and a scanner.

Our fingerprints were on file, so confirming only took seconds. A swab for our DNA was just a formality. The tech used a roller to sample the fibers from our clothes and then said we could go.

"One more thing," David said. "Charity, hand over your car keys. We need to stay together. I'll get a uniform to pick up your car and deliver it home."

My preference was to leave it at the RCMP building or the jail, but I wasn't going to waste time arguing. I could always grab a cab if I needed to be mobile without an escort.

7

W hen we pulled into the parking lot, David called his friend to let him know we were about to come get the patient.

"He'll meet us at the door," David said after ending the call. "McCarthy is in a private room. The doctor is patching him up now."

Separating Viktor from the rest of the patients was smart. We wouldn't need to deal with an audience, or a pack of potential hostages. And not working while people coughed and puked and spread their germs was a gift.

A guy in scrubs was waving to us. David got out and pulled his weapon from the locked case in the trunk.

"You think you'll need that?" I hoped the answer was no because gunfire in a hospital with oxygen tanks, sick people, and harried health professionals didn't seem like a great scenario.

"Probably not, but it sends a message."

We joined his friend, Micha, who led us past the intake desk and through a door that read Authorized Access into a quiet area with a small waiting room and three office doors, all closed.

"Yeah, wait here. I'll see what's going on. You can't have him until we finish, right?" Micha paused until we both nodded before heading into the middle office.

"I guess that's good," I said. "Clean bill of health before we take him in. No chance of him claiming police brutality."

"He might try, but he won't get anywhere with it," David said. "I'll take photos before Micha leaves. Show how damaged he was when we took him."

It was taking a lot longer than I expected for the doctor to finish. I figured Viktor was more damaged than just a bloody nose. If he needed x-rays or some other scan, we were in for a long night.

Micha slipped through the door and came over. "It's going to take a few more minutes. He really should be checked for concussion or broken ribs. He says no. Very anxious to leave. What's he done?"

He'd been beaten badly, not just a quick punch and done. I guess his hopes of starting again had evaporated.

"Got in the way of the wrong people," David said. "Can we make him take the tests? I don't want him collapsing on us."

"No. It's up to him. But the doctor isn't pushing too hard for the tests. We checked his eyes, he's not puking or dizzy, so probably not a concussion, or not a serious one. And there's no evidence of internal bleeding when we poke and prod. Make sure you have a doctor on call anyway."

"Is there someone at the jail?" I asked. I wanted answers from Viktor, and if it was going to take hours for him to be checked out, I might as well go home or look in other places for clues.

"Yes. We'll get him processed and give him the night to

worry about what we want from him," David said. "Can we have copies of his signature on the refusal of medical services?"

"You know I can't do that without a warrant," Micah said. "I'll make sure the paperwork is available when you have the warrant or a waiver of privacy from Mr. McCarthy."

"How jacked up is he?" I'd known people who were so fired up from their adrenalin they seemed to be high. "Is he going to come quietly?"

The door opened and a tired-looking doctor joined us. "He's worn out. I gave him some painkillers and told him to wait fifteen minutes before leaving. They won't sedate him, but I don't think he has the energy to argue, let alone fight."

"Thanks," David said. "Is there an exit that doesn't lead through the ER waiting area?"

The doctor looked at Micha and then headed back through the doors to the next patient.

"I'm not going to escort you," Micha said. "I've got work to do. If you keep going down this corridor, you'll find another door that drops you into the lobby." He followed the doctor back to work.

"Ready?" David asked. "We want to cuff him in the office where we can control his movements."

I nodded and let him go ahead. Inside, Viktor McCarthy was sitting on the bed and checking his phone. He had a couple of black eyes in his future and a big bruise on his jaw, but I didn't notice any broken skin or bones other than his very swollen nose, probably the source of the blood. This was a message. Viktor was done with the gang, and if he tried to get back in, the next meeting would be fatal.

"What the fuck do you want?" he asked, although his swollen lips and bruised jaw distorted the words.

"Viktor McCarthy, I am arresting you for the offense of

people trafficking. You have the right to retain and instruct counsel without delay or ask for free legal counsel. Do you understand?"

The fire went out of Viktor's eyes. "Yes. I understand."

"Do you want to call a lawyer?"

He rolled his eyes. "The only lawyer I know is paid for by someone who ordered this beating. So, I need to think about that."

David cuffed him gently and then opened the door. The area was still deserted so we marched him through the door to the lobby and out to the car.

"If I remove the cuffs so you can get in and pull on the seatbelt, will you make trouble?" David asked.

"Will you trust me if I say no? I can't fight you, but maybe I can run?"

"You'll make it to the next car before we grab you," I said. "I don't have to be gentle with you."

"Can you get in the back seat with the cuffs on?" David pulled the door open.

Viktor slid into the car and settled himself. I reached around him to click the seatbelt, ready to pull away at the slightest movement. He jerked forward as if to head-butt me, but I dodged.

"You really want to hit your head against something again?" I asked. "You'll hurt yourself more than me."

He grunted and sat back.

I secured him.

His processing, which included an examination by the doctor on duty, a review of the photos we took in the office, and a few more readings of his rights, took almost two hours. Our rules are very different from the Miranda rights everyone watches on TV, but he still had some rights. Viktor was taken away, and then we sat through an interview by the sergeant responsible for booking.

I hated all this procedure, but in the end, I was so tired that the delay felt like a bonus.

8

Viktor spent the night in jail and in the morning, the doctor cleared him for an interview. We sat in Andy's office with coffee and donuts. We weren't waiting for Viktor to be brought up to the interrogation room like I wanted. No. We were planning the strategy.

"Why don't we just wing it?" I asked. "We want him to spill something to link us to Kuznetsov. We give him a nice deal and he talks. That's all the planning we need to do."

Andy sighed like we'd been arguing for hours, not just ten minutes. "He's asked for a lawyer. We need to make sure we go about this the right way. Until his counsel arrives, we don't talk to him."

"He said he didn't know any." Viktor had sounded defeated last night with that statement, like he just realized his whole support system was owned by Kuznetsov. We should have talked to him right then and there.

"Legal Aid," David said. "He wants to be as far away from the mob lawyers as possible."

"So, you can't talk to him until the lawyer shows up? What about me?"

"We can ask him any questions we want," David said. "It's not America. He doesn't have to answer us, but we don't need to wait for counsel. It just makes it easier if we start with representation in the room. If not, they'll demand copies of the interview and any other request to delay us getting what we want. You haven't been in an interview, right? Or observed one?"

Not a real one. "No. So do I play the stupid cop?"

That made Andy laugh. "Not a cop."

"Yeah, not a cop when I want to do the fun stuff. And a cop when I want to do other fun stuff." If I thought I had any chance of getting Kuznetsov without Andy and David, I'd walk away from this arrangement and dive right into the searching without a warrant. At least the pay was good — and I got to hang out with David way more than when I worked on my own.

"You can observe," Andy said. "If you have any questions, or ideas, you can communicate through an earbud."

Better than nothing, I guess. If all I was allowed to do was observe, I didn't need to know the approach they were planning. I wasn't feeling magnanimous enough to admit that to them. "So, who's the good cop and who's the bad one?"

They shared a look and Andy nodded. I felt like I was watching partners who'd worked together for years. But that couldn't be the case. It must be some baseline cop sense that gave them the shorthand.

"I think the best way to get him to talk is to sympathize with his position," David said. "He has no good option, right? He can't go back to his life of crime. He can't protect his wife even if he wants to. He probably doesn't know how to live life straight. And he's used to the glamor of the big game."

Sympathy might work on me if they put things that way. "You can offer him a fresh start. Find Cynthia and solve his problems."

"If he doesn't buy it, there are threats," Andy said. "Like tossing him back on the streets."

I guess it made sense not to lay out the entire interview for me. It would go on its own track at some point. But at least I would know how they were playing him. I wouldn't get tied up in knots wondering what they were doing. And the reminder about Cynthia gave me something to work on. I could find her. Maybe she would have some answers.

"So, why are we waiting around?" The jail was only ten minutes by car. I grabbed my bag and jacket. "Let's go."

Neither of them moved.

"What did I miss? I'm not fighting you on the observation thing. You have your strategy."

"We need confirmation on a deal," Andy said. "I talked to the Crown Council and we're waiting for her answer."

Cop work seemed to be a lot of waiting. I put my bag down. "Do we need to wait here?"

David's phone buzzed. He checked the text. "They'll move McCarthy to an interview room in ten."

"If we don't have our answer by then, we'll head out," Andy said. "We can let him stew. If counsel shows up, he can get some advice."

This would be the last time I'd agree to work within the rules. When we had Kuznetsov locked up, I was going back to my usual cases. Boring, but in my control. I stared out the window at the office across the alley. It was an old brick building. Pigeons strutted back and forth on his window ledge.

Andy's phone rang. "Yes. Thank you." He hung up and reached for his jacket. "We've got the deal ready. McCarthy tells us something we can use to take down his old boss; he gets a new identity along with his wife."

My boredom evaporated now that we had the go ahead. This was going to work. The case could be tied up by the end of the week. I'd be back doing my own thing, investigating insurance fraud, or finding heirs to an estate. The world would be a better place for me without rules and Russian Mob bosses in it.

9

I 'd only been to the jail a couple of times. Most of my work involved finding a problem, but I'd had to bail out a couple of clients when they decided to take justice into their own hands.

The place was bleak, all yellow-beige and gray tiles. The cells were a long way from the interview rooms, but there was an odor of desperation in the air. Like too many people found their rock bottom in the building.

A few lawyers sat in the waiting area checking files or phones. No one looked up when we entered. The officer in charge was behind a plexiglass barrier, a phone beside him and a computer screen in front.

"We're here to interview Viktor McCarthy," Andy said. "We need a room."

The man behind the barrier nodded. "Take room fifteen. Down the hall. Cameras are working." He pushed a clipboard through to Andy. "Sign in. All of you."

"Has his lawyer been?" David asked.

"Here and gone about ten minutes ago." This guy clearly

didn't want to interact with anyone. "You want her back, then you call her when you get into the room."

Why would he send the lawyer away? Maybe a delaying tactic?

David signed the form and handed the clipboard to me. I filled in the questions about my identity, added my PI license number and signed.

"Was he transferred back to the cells yet?" I asked.

"Not yet. It's busy so he's still in the room she used. I figured you wanted a nicer place than I gave her, but that's still being cleaned."

He got to play petty games with the lawyers and prisoners. Lucky he liked us, or we might be in a cramped room with no seating and no air.

Andy checked his watch. "If it's busy, can we bring him into room fifteen instead of waiting?"

"No. We transport our criminals."

David touched my arm. Probably to tell me not to argue.

"Are the cameras working in that room?" Andy asked. "After he spoke to counsel, obviously."

"On the fritz. He's cuffed to the table, don't worry. No big jail break about to happen."

"We'll take a look in on him, anyway," David said, "so he knows we're waiting. Give him a chance to call his lawyer back."

I didn't get much chance to interrogate people, but I enjoyed learning the tricks just on the off chance. Keeping the subject off balance was complicated. If I was cuffed to a table in an interview room, I wouldn't let my legal representative go. If the cops put their heads in to check on me, I might feel grateful that they were going to start the interview, and that the wait was over. But then, I wouldn't be in the room after selling kids. That might make you read situations differently.

Viktor was in room three. David told me to wait outside, but I couldn't resist peeking as soon as they were both inside. Viktor was slumped over the table. His hands were cuffed to a bar, cradling his head. It didn't smell great inside, another reason to be grateful we had a better room.

Andy bent over Viktor and shook his shoulder.

Viktor's head flopped onto the table; his face turned to me like an accusation. Dead.

David hit a red button on the wall and pointed me to the hall. "Stay out of the way until we have this sorted out."

I pressed my back into the opposite wall and made myself as thin as possible. No way was I going to miss out on this. Someone had killed our best lead to Ivan Kuznetsov. I had a hard time dredging up any pity for the corpse. He bought and sold kids for a living. I saved my sympathy for the people who Kuznetsov would damage while we found our next lead.

Two EMTs ran past me into the room. I heard Andy say Viktor was dead, but they checked and called for a doctor to declare time of death.

The cop from the front desk strolled up, gave me a glare and tried to enter the room. The EMTs blocked the way. "Doctor first," the woman said.

"And no one else until we get a crime scene team in here," Andy said. "They'll be here soon. Until then, I want any recordings. And all the sign-ins starting half an hour before the lawyer arrived."

David stepped around the EMTs and joined me. "You don't need to stay," he said. "This is going to produce a lot of paperwork, and you were with us, so your statement can wait. "

"You think someone working here killed him?" Had Kuznetsov found him that fast?

"It's a closed system," David said. "Only so many people can get to a prisoner, so it's likely. We'll find the evidence and see what we can work out."

A tired looking woman in a worn lab coat walked to the door. The EMTs stepped aside. I heard Andy greet the doctor, and two minutes later she left.

The EMTs walked away after promising to hang around to give their statements and exclusion prints.

Now it was only me, David, Andy, and the guy from the front desk. Andy joined us in the hall, closing the door to the interview room.

"You'll pull the records I requested?" Andy asked the cop. "Now."

I thought the cop was going to argue, but David stepped toward him. "I'll give you a hand." They left me and Andy guarding the crime scene.

"So, what killed him?" I asked.

"Knife to the gut. Whoever did it left the blade in, so not much blood. But there might be something else we can't see until they do an autopsy."

I waited for him to tell me to go home, but he just sighed and rubbed his temples before leaning against the wall beside me.

"Does this happen often? Murder in jail?"

"Often? No, and when it does, it's in a cell, not an interview room. Yeah, someone will settle a beef with a shiv if no one is looking. That's not what happened here."

"So, Kuznetsov is our likely suspect?" *Who else would care?*

"We're not going to find him on camera or signing in.

He'd hire someone. We need to talk to the lawyer. McCarthy must have been alive when she left."

I didn't have the same confidence as Andy about that. Lawyers could be turned as easily as anyone.

"I can hear you thinking," Andy said. "Yeah, he only had one visitor. The thing is, no matter who came in, they should have been searched. Someone got through to an interview room with a knife. That means it's more than just a murder."

10

The crime scene techs showed up right after. One of them said hi to me. I think I recognized him, but he was in a hazmat-style suit, so his face was covered in a mask and his body just looked plump and crinkly white. I smiled back and then followed David to a small office away from the hustle of the investigation.

"Any results from the warehouse?" David asked. "I don't want to sit and wait for permission to continue."

"If you are feeling brave, you can ask." Andy motioned me to a chair as David left to talk to the crime scene techs. "We could be here for a couple of hours, Charity. You might as well get comfortable."

Metal folding chairs and a table with a bar for handcuffs wasn't what I thought of when I imagined comfort. "Maybe I can get coffee?"

'Water is probably a better option. The coffee here is undrinkable, and if you leave the building, I'm not sure you'll be allowed back in."

"Someone will need to interview me," I said. "I was there when you found him."

"It doesn't have to be done here," Andy said. "Your elimination prints and DNA are in the system from the warehouse. You can go home if you want."

Not a chance.

I sat and pulled out my phone. "Maybe we'll find something. I can do some work while we wait." I tried to say it like the work was unrelated to this case. Like I was a big-time investigator with more than one job underway at the same time.

"Up to you." He sat across from me.

I flipped through some Facebook posts, not expecting to find anything useful on Cynthia. She'd be in hiding and probably didn't have a clue Viktor was in jail, let alone dead.

David came back to the room a half hour later with a tray of coffee and donuts from Timmies.

"Life saver," I said. "I guess having a badge makes it easier for you to get back into the building."

"Hard to keep me out," he said. "Nothing interesting in the warehouse yet. The techs found a couple of fresh needle marks on McCarthy's forearm. Like someone drugged him before stabbing."

"So, he wouldn't make noise? Maybe no one in the building was complicit, simply careless in the safety measures. Anything else?"

"No prints on the chair or table, just some smudges. The killer wore gloves."

Andy took his phone to the hall.

"What happens now?" A murder investigation was going to get in the way of catching Kuznetsov. My gut said he ordered the killing, and we'd have a hard time proving it.

"This is going to be tricky. We need anything the murder reveals, but we can't stop looking for Kuznetsov. Best bet is that VPD continues with McCarthy, and I hear all the details."

I'd met a bunch of VPD detectives on the case I worked last year. I didn't exactly make friends. More like didn't make enemies.

"You think Leigh will catch the murderer?" I'd known her since my first case. We worked well together, and I trusted her to keep me updated so I wouldn't need to rely on David or Andy for news.

"Not the lead. She doesn't have enough experience. Paul most likely if he's available, and only if VPD catches the case. It could go to OCI; they run investigations in the jails. Or it could go to another RCMP team, since it's linked to organized crime."

Now I wanted the case to be ours. If we didn't at least put someone on the team, we'd lose any connection to Kuznetsov. This is how people like him keep operating. Distracting the cops so they can't get a real handle on you seems to be the standard method. Even if they lost a few low-level people along the way.

"What would it take for us to investigate the murder? I mean, we don't have another lead right now, so we could."

Andy walked back into the room as I asked, grabbing a coffee. "I just made that case to Michel. He's thinking about it, but, Charity, he doesn't like having a civilian on this."

Michel Benoit was Andy's boss, an officious little asshole who didn't seem to warm to me. He pushed me off the case before when I was working with Glenda Blackhouse. It hadn't kept me away. "Why? It's not like this is the first murder attached to Kuznetsov. Why is it a problem now?"

"If someone can get to a prisoner and leave no trace, it's too dangerous."

Was he telling me his opinion or quoting his boss? I

looked at David, hoping to find support, but he only looked back. I know I told him I could handle my own problems, but it would be nice to know he was on my side.

"You don't know how it happened," I said. "Maybe no one got in. Maybe after his lawyer left, some crooked guard killed Viktor."

"He hasn't ordered me to take you off the case. If he really wants you gone, he'll tell me. Michel isn't the subtext kind of manager."

My mind sorted through the options. Say nothing and wait for the order to leave, or leave now by my own choice. There were probably more, but I got stuck on these two. If I left it to Michel, he'd kick me off at the worst possible time. Either by luck or on purpose. Maybe it would come down to giving Andy a choice: me or the murder investigation. I didn't want to put either of them in that position.

"I should probably head out before I learn anything about the murder. You can call me if I'm still on the case." I picked up my jacket, leaned over to kiss David on the cheek and left before anyone tried to convince me to stay or, more likely, agree it was a good idea.

I didn't resent my position. In fact, I had to struggle to keep the smile off my face. If I wasn't part of the team, I didn't need to follow their stupid rules. I might not be able to take down a crime boss on my own, but I could ask questions about Viktor's murder, and maybe find Viktor's wife. If I learned enough, I might decide to buy my way back on the team.

11

I didn't care if Andy believed I was walking away from the case, but I did feel guilty letting David think it. I wondered why Michel kept kicking me off investigations. We met once during the Blackhouse case, and so far on this one, I'd managed to avoid bumping into him. If he didn't learn what happened from the first time, I didn't see the need to point it out.

On the last case, I kept working because I had a client. Glenda Blackhouse didn't deserve the beating, but maybe if I was still trying to get along with the authorities, they would never have found the Guptas and closed down the people trafficking operation. Alan Blackhouse got a deal for protection in exchange for him spilling secrets on Kuznetsov's organization.

He hadn't been overly eager to start talking. Although, by now, surely, he would have told them something useful.

By the time I was out on Cordova Street, I'd worked up a head of righteous indignation and a plan. The most likely place for cops to hang out around here was the Ovaltine

Cafe two blocks away on Hastings. Maybe I would find someone with information to help us.

My car was safely parked at Andy's office, so I walked the two blocks thinking through how I would get someone to tell me everything. Even when I had no idea who would even talk, or what I hoped to learn other than how Viktor's killer got access. With that, I could prove I was useful, so I'd be able to take Kuznetsov down and then never work within rules and regulations again. Yes, I know, that kind of thinking is the first step on a road to trouble, but I liked to think of it as motivation.

Inside the café, the aroma of fried bacon, mushroom, something herby, and coffee wrapped itself around me and drew me to a stool at the counter. There were only a few booths filled so I didn't need to sort through a babble of conversations to find the topic I wanted to eavesdrop on.

"Coffee," I said when the waitress arrived. "And I see you have Lemon Meringue pie."

She poured me a mug and went to grab my slice. This was supposed to be one of the best cafes in the world, according to the newspaper articles stuck to the wall. If a hole in the wall on Hastings Street was the best they could come up with, it didn't bode well for that list, but then the pie was heavenly, and the decor would be called retro if it wasn't the original. I vowed to come more often.

"You were at the jail earlier." The voice belonged to a woman who plunked down on the stool next to me. She was in her fifties, thin, and tired. "When that guy got killed, right?"

I nodded and held out my hand to shake. "Charity Deacon."

"Iris," she said. "You a fed?"

I explained I was working as a consultant. "Were you on

duty?" I asked, although the fact she was in uniform signaled the answer.

"Yeah. I'm on my way home after I finish my coffee. Going on vacation."

"Okay," I said. She wanted to tell me something, but I didn't want to get her back up by being pushy.

"Yeah, and I don't want to be interrupted when I'm off," she said. "Happens all the time, but I need this break."

"Why would they interrupt you?" If she had information, she would have given a statement.

"Well, they were still bitching over jurisdiction. I tried to give a statement to Bryce, the guy on the desk, but he said to wait for the experts."

That guy was a true jackass. "Okay, you want me to do it? Or I can introduce you to one of my team. They'll talk to you even if the case is assigned to someone else."

She shifted to a more comfortable position on the chair. The waitress placed a plate of breakfast in front of Iris and then left us alone. "The guy had a visitor. Not the lawyer. Before that. A woman. Didn't see her, so don't ask me to describe her other than short-ish, slim, dressed in dark colors, hair hidden under a scarf."

"Why didn't that show up on the log-in register?"

She dipped the point of her toast into her egg yolk. "There's ways. If you know the right people, they bring you in."

If she came in before the lawyer, this mystery person couldn't be the killer. I kept that to myself. "Anyone I should talk to?"

"I'm not going to get this guy in trouble. You need to figure out who did it. But that lawyer? The one who signed in? Looked a lot like the first woman."

Why would someone visit an inmate twice?

"Are you sure the mystery woman was in the room first?" I finished my pie and pulled out my phone to pay. "Or that someone didn't go in after the lawyer?"

"Yes, she was first. And no, I didn't see anyone else, but I didn't pay a lot of attention." She looked up from the food on her plate. "It's weird, right? If the lawyer wanted to talk to her client, she wouldn't need to sneak in. And then she came anyway."

"Yes, weird's a good word. Where are you going on vacation?"

"Hawaii. I leave tomorrow. Do I get to enjoy it?"

I couldn't guarantee it, but she knew that. "I'll mention it. Maybe the investigators can talk to you before you go."

She sighed and pushed her hash browns into a pool of ketchup. "It was worth a try."

"Are you sure the prisoner was there when the first woman went in?"

She looked at me again, a smile creeping on her face. "Good question. I'm not. It would take some of the weird out, right? If she was hiding a weapon or something."

If someone is giving unauthorized access to prisoners, I can't see why they wouldn't hide a weapon for them too. "Did you happen to notice what time the woman went in?"

"I've been counting the minutes until my vacation starts. I saw her at ten-thirty. Just an hour more of my shift left."

And twenty minutes before the lawyer signed in. Now I had something none of the official investigators had. I wouldn't hold out, but I needed a pause to get my smug under control.

"Have a great vacation," I said, getting the waitress's attention. I paid for Iris's meal too.

12

I went back to the jail and talked my way through the new desk duty guy to the small room where David and Andy were still working.

"I thought you were going home," Andy said.

David kept his eyes on the report he was reading. Too early for the crime scene findings, so maybe there was something else.

"Anything new?"

"Not yet. We've got the sign-in sheets and the videos," David said. "Nothing obvious, but a few names are worth following up on."

"Do the cameras cover the entire facility?" I didn't want to blurt out what I'd learned. Iris might have been setting me up. I didn't think so, but there was a possibility.

"The public areas. Why?" Andy asked.

"I might have something." I told them what Iris passed on. "So, this place must have corridors that only the guards use. Like at Royal Columbian. If the cameras don't cover the area, it provides a way for someone to slip in and do something without being seen."

Andy pulled up the video and ran it at high speed. "No, just the public areas."

David called the front guard to find out if there were more cameras. He grunted and hung up. "They are on the fritz. Since this morning, coincidentally."

"So, how can we use this information?" It was too much to believe some bent guard would carry out his orders knowing he was being surveilled.

"We'll do background on the guards on duty," Andy said. "This source, should we bring her in for questioning?"

That would piss her off more than intimidate her into giving us a name, and maybe she didn't know who escorted the killer in. If that's what happened. "You can interview her, but don't bring her in. She's leaving on vacation, so call her soon."

"You sure she's not the problem?" Andy asked. "Trying to shift focus until she leaves town?"

"I don't think so. Maybe she turned a blind eye but now it's resulted in a murder, she can't keep it quiet. The vacation was planned, so maybe she's hoping it blows over before she comes back? But it's probably more than one person, right? Unless our guard knows how to screw up the cameras, there's a techie involved."

David stood. "I'll go get the files for the guards on duty. We can call your source right away."

"Ask for the footage of the employee areas too," I said. "Maybe it's not blank. 'On the fritz' might mean anything."

Andy chuckled. "If you think we can restore an image out of static, you're watching too much TV. But it's worth a look."

I wanted one of those murder boards to make a note of everything. "How much longer do you need to stick around?"

"We can go anytime, but I wanted to be here." Andy picked up the copies of files and records to put them in a stack. "This changes things. Maybe we should head out as soon as David gets back. Interview your guard away from here where someone might be listening."

"Do we know who's investigating the murder?" I wasn't going to agree to leave the scene again until we knew there would be a line of communication. I'd given up the idea we should investigate because that might be what Kuznetsov wanted: us distracted by a murder. If Paul Grewal got the case, he might not like me, but David was a colleague and he'd pass on the information we needed.

"Only that it's not us," Andy said. "We can always come back if we need something, Charity. Let's not piss off Benoit enough that he pulls you off the case and issues a memo to the entire detachment." He laughed but I didn't get the joke. His boss was capable of doing something that stupid.

David came back into the room clutching a handful of papers and a thumb drive. "You'd think they could do this on-line," he muttered. "The roster with contact information and the video. I'm pretty sure if they thought about it, I'd be holding printed out stills from the cameras."

"No point in hanging around here any longer," Andy said. "We need a crime board, and some assistants to transfer that pile of hard copies into a database."

I helped pack things into boxes and followed them out of the room. Not only would the RCMP have a crime board, they'd give us a room to spread out in. We'd be able to plan without worrying that someone was spying on us. And we wouldn't be in the way of the actual investigation. "What do we tell the team assigned to the murder? If we hand over this information, they won't let us work with it, right?"

Andy smiled. "First of all, this is an RCMP task force. I'm

not obligated to share any information. We need this to move closer to arresting Kuznetsov. Second, I'll wait to find out who catches the case. And by the time they get up to speed, we'll have a report to give them."

This was going to be tricky if the wrong person worked the case. We needed to work together to catch the murderer without turning our focus away from the bigger goal. Maybe we should be fighting for the case.

"I see that look," David said. "Don't start planning to nosy in on the murder investigation. It will work out. We'll get cooperation because they need our help as much as we need to be kept in the loop."

We put the boxes in the trunk of David's car and headed back to Andy's office. The minute we stepped inside, Andy got an order to report to Michel Benoit.

"Unpack and start sorting what we've got," he said. "I'll get us a room where we can spread out."

I watched him walk through a row of cubicles to the office at the other end. "You think he's being ordered to send me home?"

David opened his laptop and inserted the thumb drive. "It's not always all about you, Charity."

So, maybe he was. And perhaps I was being paranoid.

13

I don't know what I expected. It wasn't for Andy to return in five minutes. Maybe my automatic assumption that Benoit was an asshole needed adjustment.

"We've got a murder room," he said.

David looked up from his screen. "We caught the case?"

Andy started piling up files and photos. "No, but the team doing the investigation is reporting to us. RCMP investigation because of links to organized crime."

I helped Andy gather our stuff. It wasn't a lot, so carrying it to the new room wouldn't be a problem. No need to wait for some guy with a cart. "Do you know the investigators? Are they going to cooperate?"

He shook his head at me. "Charity, you need to stop thinking everyone is a barrier. Yes, I know them. They are good. They will share and work with us."

I interpreted that to mean we could investigate the murder until it was no longer useful as a link to Kuznetsov. I figured that would happen as soon as we solved it. I couldn't imagine that the killing was completely unconnected.

"When are they getting here?" David asked. "We need to work this lead about the visitor before it goes cold."

I followed them down the hall to a large conference room with a free-standing whiteboard and a smart screen on the wall. I dumped my armful of paperwork and pulled out a chair to wait for the answer.

"Ten minutes," Andy said. "We need to give them an update, so let's get organized. I'd like to be in on the interrogation of the guard who let a woman set up a murder. This is our best shot at getting close to Kuznetsov."

Andy and I started posting everything we had on the whiteboard while David played the video out on the smart screen. When I glanced over, I saw mostly static with a few shadows moving through. Useless except for the time codes.

"It matches my source," I said. "She told me the mystery visitor came around ten-thirty, and the screen logs the shadows at ten-thirty-two. What time did the lawyer go in?"

David checked his notes. "Signed in at ten-forty. In the room by ten-fifty. So, it could be the same person. Not a lot of time, though."

"I don't understand why the killer needed to go in ahead of time," Andy said. "Too much of a risk. But what time did they put McCarthy in the room?"

"Five minutes before the lawyer," David said. "So, it isn't possible for the first one to kill him and leave because surely the lawyer would notice her client was dead."

We'd be able to hear the real story from the bent guard, but going into that interrogation with some idea of the truth would help break him. "Can we see when the shadow leaves? I mean, if it's the same person as the lawyer, they did what they needed to do and got back to sign in, all within eight minutes."

David ran the video again. It was like staring at one of

those 3-D pictures that were popular for a while. I couldn't be sure whether I was seeing actual movement on the screen, or if my brain, trying to make sense of the image, tried filling in bits.

"Let's make sure we agree on what happened," I said. "I think the guard stayed in the hall. The visitor went in, and a minute later they came out." If my brain was playing tricks, no one else should have seen the same thing.

"Yeah. And the visitor is a lot shorter than the guard," Andy said. "If we had more detail it might help, but I couldn't make out anything like the door height, so no guess on if we have a very tall guard or a very short killer."

Before we could poke at the tiny amount of data again, a man and a woman joined us.

"Good," Andy said. "Time for introductions and an update."

The woman, Gena Hunt, medium height, brown hair, brown eyes, perfect for undercover if that was her role, and the man, Luc Moulin, tall, thin, graying hair, and blue eyes, sat and listened while Andy gave the update.

"So, we have a puzzle, yes?" Luc said. "This man McCarthy is a confederate of Ivan Kuznetsov, and you believe his death is a hit."

"I'd be very surprised if it was about something else," I said. "We are going after the bent guard."

Luc gave me a slow nod and then spoke to Andy. "Then we must build a trap. For today, the same time? Perhaps the same people will be on shift."

"Except your source," Gena said.

"She's away," I said. "If we need to contact her, please let me do it." We had a few hours before Iris got on the plane. I didn't want her hounded by someone when she landed.

"And it is too early to set our trap," Luc said. "You have

been working a long shift. Perhaps we can organize ourselves, then you leave Gena and I to sort through what is here. To find out if the same people are on shift, so we may set up interviews, I believe will be the best excuse for asking. Is the attitude cooperative at the jail?"

"Not eagerly so, but yes, I think you might need to placate some egos." Andy shuffled some papers into a pile on the desk.

As soon as Luc said we should go, my eyes started to droop. I'd been awake almost twenty-four hours. "Okay," I said. "We could do with a few hours' sleep."

"Luc and I will come up with something to trap our bent guard," Gena said. "Off the top of my head, I say we lie about being able to reconstruct our video. It will only frighten the person who let this stranger in the back door."

David grabbed his coat and beckoned me to join him. "We'll be back in four hours. That should give us time to recharge and still get ready to catch a bad guy."

Andy stayed behind to pass on a few more details. David and I headed for the street. He pulled me toward the car and took my keys. "You look like you're about to pass out," he said. "They'll do fine, and with Luc and Gena starting now, we'll have easy twenty-four-hour coverage."

I tried to believe it would work. That the two investigations would sync, but I couldn't. Maybe things would be fine for Andy and David, but I was an outsider. I'd still be working my own ideas at some point.

14

The trap sounded pretty simple. Start with a background check to find the weak point, and then get an undercover cop to pay for access just like the killer did. No one needed me for the operation. I wanted to be there for the take-down, but not for the waiting around.

What I wanted to do was find the killer. Yes, finding the bent guard would be a step forward, but not necessarily in the direction we needed. What if they only took money to bring the killer in? What if they couldn't identify the mystery visitor beyond what we already knew? Maybe they had some information to share, maybe not. If I was a bent guard, I'd make sure I had some insurance for leverage. That insurance might be our link to Kuznetsov. I mean, who else wanted the man dead?

If this was Kuznetsov cleaning house, we'd find a lot more bodies soon, and each one would be another locked door in our search for evidence. Kuznetsov's henchmen might not have the right skills. This was surgical — no bystanders, no witnesses, no evidence —and the members of Kuznetsov's team I'd met seemed more likely to shoot the place up than kill one man quietly. This must be a professional killer.

When I suggested we look for local hitmen, okay and hitwomen, Andy said it would take too long. If we had a better description of the killer, we'd be able to target the right one. That is, if they were still around. Pros tended to fulfill the contract and move on before anyone could catch them.

I didn't argue, but I believed it was more likely that Kuznetsov would keep a good assassin around until we had multiple deaths to deal with. Being in protective custody wouldn't stop a good killer finding Alan Blackhouse or the Guptas. Or Cynthia Towers, Viktor's wife. Or me, I guess.

"I'll see you later," I said as I headed out. I didn't want to tell anyone where I planned to go, or why. I didn't have a plan worked out in any detail, so I expected to be told to stay if I tried to explain.

When I got to my car, my phone pinged. A text from David. *Be careful.*

I sent back a smiley face.

Now the fact that my plan ran short on the details got important. I had no idea how to go looking for a professional killer. I knew the dark web was a marketplace, but there had to be some other way. Not everyone who wanted to bump off a partner or rival had TOR access. Anyone could download the app easily. Getting an invitation to a site for illegal transactions probably only came through people you knew. So, a wife looking to bump off her asshole husband, or stalker, or rich, old sugar daddy, needed a clean way to find someone.

Guy was my usual contact in the shady world. I'm not

sure he'd be happy to point me to a specific killer, but maybe he would tell me who the local people were.

He didn't respond to my text requesting to meet, so I had to keep going on my own. The next choice was some shifty dive bar. Andy's building wasn't far from a seedy part of Vancouver. I would leave my car in the RCMP lot, no point in moving it to different parking spaces and risk losing parts along the way.

My phone pinged a text. Guy: *Not today. Call you tomorrow morning.*

I sent a thumbs up emoji and headed north toward the less well-known areas of the Downtown Eastside.

There were a couple of bars near the water where I could get a beer and a taco, and maybe a conversation. The first one was behind a door with chipped black paint. *The Blowhole* held a collection of old men huddled over half-drunk beers at one table, and some tattooed hard-asses with shot glasses filling the tabletop at another. It smelled like they'd decided to comply with the smoking ban five minutes ago. The bartender was watching a soccer game on the TV and didn't even turn to see who'd entered.

"Gabe, how about a special?" I asked. The special; a shot of water poured from a vodka bottle.

Gabe and I went way back. He served some time in federal prison and swore he never wanted to go back. That didn't mean he got straight. Not too many employers were eager to hire someone with his resume. The bar was his first job after getting out, and he'd been here fifteen years.

"Long time," Gabe said as he filled my order.

No one seemed to be paying us attention. I must be too old to be harassed by the tattooed crowd. Or they respected Gabe enough to leave me alone.

I dropped my voice because I didn't believe we were being ignored. "Not really my kind of place."

"Your new boyfriend prefer you to stay on the narrow?"

"I would never let him learn about you," I said. "He's learned to let me live my life."

Gabe glanced at the screen again as the announcer dragged out the word 'goal.' He shrugged and turned back to me. "What are you looking for?"

"My case involves a bit more grit than usual. Do you know how someone would hire a killer?"

He stepped back, picked up a dingy cloth and started polishing a glass. I let him digest my question. Gabe never told me to be safe; he sometimes lied about knowing stuff, but I'd always figured it was more about keeping his ass safe than mine. I liked that about him.

"What's your interest?" he finally asked.

"Trying to track down someone who hired a hit."

He picked up another glass and applied the cloth. It was actually bringing a shine up, so maybe not as dirty as it looked.

"Who's the client?"

"I suspect someone, but it's probably good that you don't hear his name."

"Not many independents in town. You think maybe a local?"

I shrugged and tossed back my water then pushed the glass to him for another. The young gangsters called for another round. Gabe filled and delivered their order. A quick exchange of words before he left their table settled them down. When he got back, he filled the shot glass with water again and leaned on the bar.

"They wanted to know if you were looking for a good time."

I forced myself not to look at the table. "Can't imagine any of them knowing how to give me one."

"The contract filled?" I nodded and Gabe asked, "What kind of kill?"

"Surgical. Stabbed and not much blood. Knife left behind."

"Not a local then." Gabe pointed to my glass, so I tossed it back. "I don't know any outside talent. Pay up and leave before those guys get drunk enough to ignore my warning."

I tossed twenty dollars on the counter. "Thanks."

If Kuznetsov brought in a killer, I was pretty sure none of my contacts in the other bars would know who it was either.

15

D avid sent me a text to meet at the jail. The plan was in place, and we were about to catch our first suspect — the first one still living, anyway.

The undercover operative turned out to be a young-looking agent. I noticed her lurking around the back of the jail as I passed. She wore a cheap gray suit and blouse, her hair tied back in a ponytail, and flat black shoes. Someone playing a role. I guess she meant to lull our target into not asking too many questions. Dressing like a junkie wouldn't give the right impression. Money and power behind a desperate front were just the kind of go-between Kuznetsov would use.

David waited for me at the front door. He hurried me past the registration desk and into the same office we used before. "Gena and Luc will be interviewing one of the men in McCarthy's cell. The UC will try to get in first with a warning to keep quiet."

"We won't be able to do that more than once. How many suspects do we have?" No matter how slick the plan was, word would get around. If our first shot didn't pan out, we were unlikely to succeed with a second pass. "And where is Andy?"

"Waiting in with Gena and Luc. It would be better if he was in the interview room when the UC enters, but we aren't sure about any of the people working here right now."

At least we wouldn't be finding a dead body today. "And how many suspects?"

"Two. We reviewed the roster and confirmed it was correct. Two men who fit the general size of the staticky blur we saw before. One of them called in sick. He's under observation until we finish here."

"How long?" It didn't feel like we were doing any good sitting in a room when all the action was happening outside. I couldn't argue with the logic; we had no role in the murder investigation. Gena and Luc were the official investigators; Andy was supervising. No room for lookie-loos. "How can we be sure it worked?"

"We should know in ten minutes. The UC will text us, then start her end of the operation. If it's the right guy, he'll be in here with us, waiting for transport to the RCMP lockup. If he's not, we'll head out after the other guard."

"I need some names," I said. "Can we call the UC something? Who is the guard we're trapping? Who's the other guy?"

He nodded like he suddenly remembered I wasn't part of the official team and didn't understand the rules. "We call the UC that because we don't want to accidentally use a name. She's taking this time away from her long-term gig, and we need to keep her separate. The guy we're trapping is Dean Marshall. It looks like he's being blackmailed for something."

Okay, I had to trust they knew what being blackmailed looked like. I'd find out the details later on the other guard. If he was innocent, I didn't need to know why we suspected him. There could be more than this one who's not up front about a shady connection, but we only needed one.

David's phone pinged with the text. "Okay, only a few minutes now."

"So, she's waiting for this Dean guy to show up so she can proposition him?" No way would she send a text after making contact. Or maybe she had that planned into her cover.

"He went out for a smoke break," David said, "but he doesn't smoke. I guess he's used to meeting someone out back."

Likely to do with whatever the blackmail was about. I guess if you've gone so far as to be a tool for some criminal, you have no incentive to stop what you were doing. "What if he doesn't bite?" The waiting was getting to me. My brain knew the operation would take no more than a few minutes, but it felt like we'd been waiting an hour.

"We would have another text. Either she's negotiating, or threatening, or we're about to meet Mr. Marshall."

How can he be so calm? I itched to go peek into the corridor leading to the interview rooms.

"You think he'll talk?"

"Eventually," David said. "We just need to find a way to make it happen today. Andy is good at interrogation, don't worry."

Another interview I'd be relegated to observing.

The door opened and Andy pushed a tall man in his mid-fifties into the room; almost totally bald, with blotches of anger or shame... or fear burned on his cheeks.

"Sit down." Andy gave Dean Marshall a shove toward the empty chair. "You can talk now, save us a lot of time and maybe gain you a better deal, or you can make me work for it and lose any chance at a future outside prison. Conspiracy to commit murder comes with a long sentence."

Dean slumped but didn't speak. Andy and David stood beside the chair; a bit too close for anyone's comfort. I didn't move or even think about asking questions. I didn't want to break the menacing mood, and also, I had this almost undeniable need to spit out all my secrets.

"Okay, keep quiet if you think that's your best shot," Andy said. "You'll be transferred to the federal holding center where you'll be interviewed and charged with aiding and abetting a murder for hire."

Dean didn't react.

"If you tell us what you know now, I have an offer of leniency from the Crown Council."

Dean looked up at Andy but didn't speak.

"Someone read you your rights?" David asked. Dean nodded. "Do you want legal representation?"

Dean shook his head.

I guess he figured the last guy didn't fare too well with his lawyer.

Someone knocked on the door. Andy opened it and two uniformed RCMP constables walked up to the chair, ordered Dean to stand, and marched him out.

"How long before the deal goes away?" I asked.

Andy checked his phone. "If he talks, he gets the deal. I'm not sure our approach is going to work the fastest. He's too scared."

If someone called in an expert, we'd all be sitting in the observation room.

Andy put his phone away. "I think you should try, Charity. He knows you're involved with us, but he might open up to some sympathy."

I laughed at the idea I might be considered the sympathetic one. "Happy to try."

16

The interview room was big enough to hold a table with two chairs on each side. The obligatory one-way mirror covered the top half of the wall behind where I sat so the perp could be under observation. A camera watched from the ceiling, but no red light, so it must be off. There didn't seem to be any controls for the camera, so maybe it was on, and the light had been disabled.

Dean Marshall sat across from me, his breathing ragged. He didn't acknowledge my presence, just sat looking at his cuffed hands.

I settled in, put my phone on the table beside me and started talking.

"Dean, are you sure you don't want a lawyer here?"

"The last lawyer I dealt with led to me being arrested."

Not much, but he was talking. I didn't need to be told the first few words were the beginning of a journey toward talking too much. "Do you want to tell me about it?" It was worth a try.

He shook his head, still keeping his eyes down.

Before I came in, David and Andy gave me some tips on

interviewing suspects. Although I guess Dean just gradu-
ated from suspect to culprit. They refused to let me play
good cop — because it's a stupid trope of mysteries, and
because I wasn't a cop. The gist of the advice was to find a
way to come across like an ally. Don't make promises to keep
him out of jail; he won't believe you. Don't play down how
dangerous it is to talk. Whoever ordered Viktor McCarthy's
murder didn't care if he talked. *Whoever*, like we didn't think
Kuznetsov put out the contract.

"You're in a bad situation," I said. "You don't have to give
me details, but do you know the person who killed that
prisoner?"

That made him look up. He glanced up at the camera
and then at me. "No. I did a job. I didn't want the details."

"Yeah. I've done a few innocent jobs that got me in trouble. You agree to do a favor and the next thing, some killer is
forcing you to take a giant step across the line. Is that what
happened?"

He nodded.

"You want some water? Coffee? Are you hungry?"

He swallowed and checked the camera again. I thought
he was going to refuse the offer.

"Water would be good."

I opened the door and asked the constable outside to
bring a couple of bottles and a bag of chips. If Dean didn't
want to eat, I could nibble.

"Refreshments on the way," I said. "You know I'm not a
cop, right?"

"What do you mean? They let you in here to question
me? Why?"

If I hadn't ordered refreshments a moment ago, I could
have said my visit wasn't sanctioned. Try to think ahead,
Charity. "I talked them into it. The cops have their agenda, I

have mine. They want you and that killer. They figure you give them the assassin, then she gives them a bigger fish."

The constable gave a knock and then opened the door without waiting for an invitation. He stared at Dean like he wanted to drag him off to a cell. The water and chips went down with a thump. "Any problems?" he asked me.

"You can go back to guard duty," I said. "Everyone is doing fine."

David and Andy were in the observation room. This guard was a version of pissed off cop. He gave a great impersonation of an official reluctant to let me talk to the prisoner. I thought the performance might be a bit heavy handed, but Dean cowered a tiny bit more while the man was in the room.

And David had made sure the chips were my favorite. I opened one of the waters and handed it to Dean. The cuffs made it awkward, but he could hold it to his lips. He drank down half the contents in one go.

I opened the chip bag down the back seam and put it between us. "Help yourself."

He shook his head again. "So, what's your agenda?"

"Sorry?"

"You said you had a different agenda. What do you want from me?"

Now that I had him engaged, I could make some headway.

"I need to protect someone. An innocent who married the wrong man. She has a kid."

"How are you planning to protect her?"

I shrugged this time. *Let him do the talking.*

After a few minutes, he lost the tension in his shoulders. Dean sat straighter in the chair and reached for a chip. Relaxing him was the goal, but watching it happen so quickly gave me the chills. Had the depressed victim all been an act? Who exactly was being played in this room?

"You figure putting the boss away will protect her, right?" He put his elbows on the table and leaned in conspiratorially.

I forced myself not to draw back, glad the cuffs held him in place. "It couldn't hurt. Do you know anything that can help me?"

"What can you do for me in return? Are you going to promise leniency? Like that other guy? There's nothing you can do to protect me if I'm on a list."

"I can't offer you anything," I said. "You know that. I can try to talk to the cops, but you need protection, and they're the only ones even thinking of offering it. Why not tell me what I need?"

He drank some more water and ate a few more chips. The entire time his eyes locked on me. I kept silent. Could this be his way of making the decision? I hoped so; otherwise, I had no idea what he was trying to communicate.

It took him long enough that I thought Andy would barge in and end the interview, but eventually Dean stopped staring at me and sat back.

"You're right. I guess you are my only hope. The bitch I let in the back door planted a knife. If you have a video of the lawyer, I can tell you if it's the same woman."

"Describe her," I said. I picked up my phone to find an image we took from the security camera. I turned on the record feature in the process, in case someone denied me access to the interview recording.

"Skinny. Blond. Sharp face, like she'd never had a good time. Blue eyes. Somewhere between late twenties and early forties. Had that look about her, you know, either a hard looking young chick or a young-looking old chick. You seen that movie about the dragon tattoo?"

I found the image on my phone. "I saw it." I held out the phone so he could see.

He leaned in. "Yeah, but not so healthy."

The picture from the security feed was in black and white. But it looked like a dark-haired, plump woman. Not enough detail to see her expression, but that could be checked with the officer who signed her in. At first glance not the same woman, but clothes can be padded, and wigs were cheap. I held it up for Dean to see.

"Looks like her ugly sister," he said.

17

As soon as I joined David and Andy in the observation room, I knew something was wrong. Dean Marshall was hunched over the table, his head resting on his fists. Thinking about, or maybe regretting, whatever led him to that room. I couldn't drum up much sympathy. He'd done something to give a killer leverage, and it wasn't a series of innocent favors.

David looked at me like he was bracing for an argument. Andy stood a few steps away, not meeting my eyes. Great. I got information for them, and they'd been planning something behind my back. Something I wouldn't like.

"You found a lead, I guess." I refused to give them an opening by asking what's up. "Confirmed that the killer and the lawyer were the same person? Or we're dealing with evil twins?"

"Thanks for that," Andy said. "We would have gotten there eventually, but you got him talking faster than I expected. We'll use the description to identify the assassin. Maybe convince her to turn on whoever hired her."

I had enough information to do a little research of my

own. Even if she was from outside, someone would know her by reputation. Assassins probably didn't use a wide range of methods. One for distance kills, poison or gun. One for close up under observation, poison or a knife.

I sat and watched Marshall through the glass. "You think he might be holding back something?"

"Gena and Luc will go in next," Andy said. "Now he's talking, it will be easier to keep him going."

David sat next to me. He didn't look at Marshall. He leaned forward, hands clasped, elbows on his knees. If I didn't trust him to let me do my thing, it might look like a setup meant to keep me from blowing up over whatever's coming next.

"Charity, we need to rethink the investigation. If Kuznetsov is starting to cut loose ends, the situation is too dangerous."

I waited a beat while my inner voice ranted about protecting myself. When I had it under control, I said, "Okay. So, I get a gun? I'll need lessons and practice. I'm not sure we have time for that."

"And I don't think anyone is ready to teach you," Andy said.

David glared at him and then turned back to me. "I know, you can take care of yourself."

"Yes. I can. I get the idea there's a big fat *but* in there."

"We can't risk a civilian getting hurt," Andy said. "I know you wanted to tell her, Anchor, but we don't have time. Charity, you're a good investigator, but you are not a cop. You did a great job getting Marshall talking, but right now, you aren't interfering in Kuznetsov's activities directly, so you're safe."

No way Ivan Kuznetsov didn't remember who I was or what I'd done to get his money launderer arrested. Part of me — a big bitchy part — wanted to argue that I should stay on the case. To point out they wouldn't be here without my work. The other more rational part wanted out. I might get further by myself. All the support and access the cops had wasn't helping me catch Kuznetsov. I longed for the old days when I used the cops for information and to call in at the last minute for the arrest.

Of course, before I met David, I used to end up in the hospital a lot. And I had people like Val and Lu, and the men in their lives as support. But Lu and Matthieu were still in France. Val and Rory were tangled up in the complications of her past and his father's reputation. I would be going alone. And despite my bravado, I had never been completely alone.

"Is this Benoit's idea?" I needed to test the boundaries of this sudden concern for my safety. "He never wanted me on this case to start with."

"A bit," David admitted. "He's management. His job is to worry about liability. It's also about me. I know I said I wouldn't stop you doing your job to keep you safe, but I think this is too dangerous for you."

I knew this moment would come. He'd find an exception to the promise to let me live my life. A spiky ball of disappointment and betrayal grew in my gut. It didn't help that he was right. This was very risky. "It's just as dangerous for you." My voice sounded small and scared. This loving someone hurt.

"I'm trained and armed. And I know when to back off," he said. "You keep pushing until something breaks."

He wasn't wrong about that. My ability to think about consequences disappeared when the case was close to cracking. "Okay. I'll stop," I said. "I don't like it, but if you don't want me on the team, you won't give me anything but busy work anyway."

"Don't be like that," David said.

"No," Andy said. "She's right. I mean, we're not prepared to lock her up to keep her safe. Maybe we should keep her on the team. We need someone to sort through paperwork and cart evidence around." His smile told me that tactic hadn't occurred to him until I mentioned it. Unfortunately for him, that kind of thing only worked until I figured it out, so it wasn't an option now.

"My stuff is in your office," I said. "I'll grab it and head out."

They exchanged glances. I had some stuff on my phone, but video content, personnel files, images would come in handy. I needed to get into the office and collect copies of everything.

"We'll call you if we think it's safe for you to carry on with us," Andy said.

"I'll see you at home," David said.

I nodded and left the observation room. No one waited outside to escort me out of the building. They knew what I was going to do and didn't care. Maybe, but all that talk about it being too risky was Michel Benoit's bullshit, and they wanted me working in the shadows. At least, they must trust me not to take any originals, just copies. I wasn't that stupid.

18

I took my treasures home with me. David wasn't going to drop by, so I could investigate to my heart's content without worry.

I made coffee and grabbed a half-empty bag of popcorn to fuel my brain. Then I sat staring at the pile of papers and the thumb drive. Nothing stood out as a place to start. I didn't have the resources to clean up the video; it didn't stop me from lying about it to someone to scare them, but all I'd ever see is a screen of fuzzy white.

I'd been running on the RCMP processes so far, and maybe that was why I was stuck. Start from the beginning — Viktor's death — and figure what I still needed to learn so I could get to Kuznetsov. I grabbed a pad of paper to make notes and flipped open the first file.

My phone buzzed. Guy.

"Hey, can you talk?"

"Would I call to say I can't talk?"

"No. I'd still be trying to get you to answer my texts."

"What did you want?"

This was going to be one of those all-business calls. I hated them because the result was mostly no information and goodbye. No opportunity to cajole, or threaten, or tease Guy past the initial refusal to get me in trouble.

"I'm looking for a contract killer."

The pause went on way too long. "You must have other options," Guy finally said. "Ask your boyfriend or your new best bud to arrest whoever pissed you off."

"You really think I would come to you to hire a killer? I don't know whether to be annoyed you don't trust me enough, or proud you think I'm a badass."

"I guess I need sleep," Guy said. "Do I want to hear the reasons?"

"A prisoner got assassinated, and I'm trying to tie the murder back to whoever ordered it." That was all the information I wanted to give. If Guy knew we were hunting Kuznetsov, he might shut me down.

"I heard something happened," he said. "I can point you to a few I know about. You should pass the names on to your boyfriend. You can't twist these guys around your finger, Charity. They don't understand remorse. Killing is a job. If they think you might get in the way of their future income stream, they know how to hide a body, or leave it out as a lesson."

For some reason, no matter how many cases I worked, Guy thought I saw the criminal world as rebel pack of Disney characters. That I had no idea of the danger I faced when I reached out. The last part was true. If I thought too much about getting killed, I'd find a nice, safe job. Too bad for him I liked being a PI.

"I won't walk up to anyone and ask if they filled any contracts lately," I said. "Give me some credit. It's probably an outside killer. Maybe they'd be happy to point me in the direction of the competition."

I caught a blast of loud voices in the background at Guy's end. It sounded like a party.

"No, they won't. I told you they don't feel shit like normal people."

"Okay, are you giving me the names or not? If you don't, someone else will." I was in no rush to end the call, but if our past discussions were a good indicator, Guy would be claiming he had to get back to the gang before someone noticed him on the phone.

"No names. Are you ready to write this down?"

I flipped to a clean page of the notepad. "Go ahead."

He streamed off five sets of numbers. "Those are the URLs to contact the usual people."

"Any of them women?"

"The middle one and the last one. Was your killer a woman?"

"No comment," I said. "The less you learn from me the better. How do you know which one to call if you want to put out a contract?"

"The Hells Angels don't put out contracts on people."

That's why he has five random URLs at hand. "Sure, you do your own work, right?"

"No comment."

Perhaps my smart mouth explained why Guy had no faith that I understood the risks. I keep reminding myself the Angels are a violent gang, and I had no guarantee that Guy could or would protect me if it came down to disobeying an order. Everyone seemed to forget that when the Angels did Christmas toy donations, the money to fund that program came from drugs and prostitution, and maybe a little arms dealing on the side.

"I'll keep your name out of it," I said. "They won't be able to track by the URL that someone in the gang sent me?"

"No. The sites change when five people use them. I have no idea if the numbers will be available for much longer. I don't know how the boss gets the new ones, and I'm not giving you those, understand?"

Yes. He was already regretting helping me. The longer we kept our relationship, the more likely the boss would find out. "I'll do what I need fast," I said.

"And don't meet anyone," he said. "If they know who you are..."

"Yeah, I'm dead."

"No. They'll try to own you first. Or sell you off to Kuznetsov. He's who you're really after, right? Think of a good story that doesn't link to your case. Ask all your questions in one contact and take no for an answer."

"I'll be safe," I assured him. I had ways of accessing these sites without leaving a trail.

Guy ended the call without a goodbye.

Now I had to find a way to keep my promise without taking too much time.

My phone buzzed. David.

"What have I done wrong now?"

"Surprisingly nothing. We want to interrogate Dean Marshall, and he's balking. He wants you in the room."

"I'm not a lawyer."

"He doesn't want one, but he won't talk to us until you arrive. He thinks you're on his side. Andy wants to know if you can keep up that appearance without interfering with the questioning."

I closed my laptop and tossed my notepad into my bag. "I'll try. When?" If I could avoid emailing contract killers by getting information from a bent guard, I'd happily do so.

"As soon as you can get here," he said. "We can send a cruiser."

"I'll call a cab." It would be faster than getting my car from the parking garage, and I'd be able to figure out how to word that email on the way.

19

I stood in the crowded observation room. David and Andy sat behind Gena and Luc, who stood. This was the part where they told me the rules. I couldn't pull my eyes away from the scene through the one-way glass.

There were three chairs on the interrogator's side of the desk. Dean looked more relaxed, but I wondered if he'd been in the room the entire time. He must know I wasn't really on his side, but then again, he'd talked to me like a friend. I'd been sympathetic, and I guess it worked better than just getting a confession.

"You don't get to ask questions," Luc said, "or interrupt us."

It sounded boring, but I nodded. If I asked a question in the room, how would they stop me? If I figured out some way to narrow down my search for professional killers, I'd be... not safer, but less at risk?

"We wanted you in here watching," Gena said, "but he's determined that you be in the room. You are not his friend. You sit on our side of the table. We want him thinking he needs to earn our trust."

"And if he refuses to talk under that kind of atmosphere?" It didn't make any difference to me, I'd do whatever helped our case, not stick to the rules.

"You can be a carrot or a stick," Gena said. "If he cooperates, he gets to keep his buddy in the room. If he balks, you go away, and he learns what a real interview feels like."

"So, you're the bad cop?"

"Charity, don't be a smart ass," David said. "You are back on the team, why push?"

I wasn't back on the team. I was back because they needed me. And if Andy decided he didn't need me again, I'd be working it alone. "What's the goal?" If we worked toward different outcomes, it would be a problem. I would not veer off my plan, but maybe we were going for the same thing.

"This guy is a poor sap who got into trouble. If he cooperates, no charges. If he doesn't, then he's in jail and the killer can get to him."

"I understand the threat. I'm pretty sure he does too. You'll protect him in jail, right?"

"Yes," Andy said. "But we can't be a hundred percent. If she wants to, the killer can get back in and take care of him. She's got a lot of incentive to close a hole."

"If he cooperates, he just goes back to work? He'll be safe?"

"No record of his arrest," David said, "and we'll put it out that he doesn't know anything. Best we can do."

Dean did involve himself in the situation, but it didn't sound like the best they could do. I kept my mouth shut for a couple of reasons. One, I trusted David. And, let's face it, the other reason was I didn't have a better option right now.

"Are you ready?" Luc asked.

"Has he eaten?" I might not get a chance to ask questions, but I could reinforce the idea I was his friend if I made an effort.

"Yes." Gena sighed and checked the time. "Fed, watered, and allowed a potty break. Can we get going?" I hoped she was staying in character because she didn't come across like this kind of hardass before.

I followed them in. Checked the seats like it was the first time I saw the arrangement. The two had left me the first chair. On the corner of the table, slightly turned and separated. So I didn't look like a cop, I guess.

Gena placed a file on the table, leaving it closed. Luc pulled out his phone and checked the screen before dropping it back in his pocket.

"Are you okay?" I asked Dean the question, garnering me a scowl from Gena.

"Yeah. Thanks for coming back."

I nodded at him and vowed to keep to the rules.

"Walk us through your day," Gena said. Dean opened his mouth, but she kept talking. "How did you know to let the woman in behind the scenes? How did you mess with the video? What were you paid?" She was putting him on edge, firing questions so fast.

Dean waited for a few beats. "I don't understand what you want. I didn't get paid. They blackmailed me."

"Have you done this before?" Luc asked.

Why didn't anyone ask who they were? Another tactic to keep him off-kilter?

"No. The first time. And the last. They said I was clear."

"Until the next time you put yourself into a position to be leveraged again. Not too many people smart enough to keep from falling into the same traps over and over again."

He rubbed his face with his cuffed hands. "I won't be that stupid again."

"You said you let the woman in to plant a knife," Gena said. "How did she tell you she was there?"

"I didn't know I was letting her in to plant that knife."

"What did you think she was going to do?" Gena asked.

"I didn't think about it."

"How did you know she'd be there?" Gena asked again.

Why is this important? If they wanted the next bigger fish, it wouldn't be a message carrier.

"A note in my locker."

Gena opened the file and made a note on the blank sheet on top. "So, someone else is being blackmailed to run errands for criminals? Who?"

"No. We have temporary guards sometimes, so someone could have pretended to be a cleaner, or whatever."

"So, you are capable of imagining facts," Gena said. "What about the video? Was that some mysterious temporary person in disguise?"

Why aren't they asking about the woman?

"It's in a locked room," Dean said. "I told the woman to keep her head down, because I know where the cameras are. That's all. I didn't take them down."

"Did you keep your eyes on her?" Now Gena was getting to the point.

"No. You think I would let her leave a knife in the room if I knew?" Dean's knee started bouncing under the table. I guess Gena's interview style had him agitated. Pushing his buttons so she could get to the real questions. "What if it had been so that McCarthy had a weapon to attack the RCMP? Someone said he sold kids. Who cares if he's dead?"

"He was a prisoner in your care," Luc said. "It doesn't matter what he's charged with."

"You say that, but we get some scum in there. Not too many innocent people occupying the cells."

"Did the woman say anything?" Gena asked.

"No. Maybe when she was playing lawyer. Ask whoever took her in." His anger simmered just below attack level.

"If you have nothing to tell us, we can't help you, Dean." Luc leaned in, playing concerned. "Did you keep the note?"

"No. I'm supposed to destroy them when I've got the message."

Gena made another note before saying, "I thought this was the first time. You've received messages before?"

He looked at me like I should do something to protect him from this aggressive woman.

"Do you have anything the cops can use to find this woman?" I asked. "We want to protect you, but it comes at a price."

"I thought you would be on my side." He hefted himself out of the chair at me, held back by the fact his cuffs were attached to a bar. "You're just another bitch."

Luc stood and faced Dean down.

When Dean sat back in his seat, I said, "If you don't know anything that can help us find the killer, no one is on your side. You asked for me to be here. You think I don't have better things to do?"

He glared at me but stayed in his seat. "Tattoo. She had a tattoo on her neck at the back. I only saw it because her scarf slipped."

Now we knew she'd been wearing a scarf the first time. Dean hadn't realized we should already have the answers because we'd looked at the surveillance video. Gena was very good at this.

"Describe the tattoo," Luc said.

"I only saw part of it. Like a bunch of dots, like someone tried to make a string of beads. Maybe the rest of it made sense."

20

I waited for someone to jump on the clue. A tattoo like a string of beads might not be unique, but it couldn't be common. If I had a question for Dean, I'd ask it, but nothing came to mind.

Gena made a 'hmm' sound. Like she was assessing whether or not the information had value. She jotted something on the page in front of her. Why didn't Dean ask about the contents of that file? Did he know it contained his previous statement and about a hundred blank pages for padding? Or was he afraid to find out that the RCMP knew about all the little favors he'd done?

Gena looked up from writing and started her act again. "What color beads? What's the significance? How tall was she compared to you?"

Dean closed his eyes and breathed deeply for a few moments. Trying to take control of the interview? To piss off Gena? To quell his panic?

"Black ink with a bit of a white spot, like to make it look like a round bead. No, I don't know shit about gang tats. The top of her head came to my shoulder, but she maybe slumped a bit."

The description helped fill out the image from the woman signing in as his lawyer. The perspective of the ceiling-mounted camera made it hard to judge height. I kept making mental notes. Maybe knowing this detail would help me glean information from the static.

"Okay," Luc said. "We can check on all of this to see how much you lied. But if we find out you held back, no deal for you."

Gena glared at Luc and Dean's face dropped as though he didn't know who to look to for support. Luc's threat had pushed him off kilter. He was grabbing for a lifeline. He looked to me and I saw the panic in his eyes; I smiled.

"I didn't leave anything out. I mean, if I did, it wasn't on purpose." He blurted out the words.

"We'll deal with that when it becomes important," Gena said, as if his excuse meant nothing. "Let's go back to earlier. Who did you do the favor for? Is it the same person? Or did someone sell off your services?"

The last question took Dean by surprise. "They do that? Criminals? Sell off their leverage?"

Gena's smile was nasty. She turned to Luc and rolled her eyes. "Now he's playing the innocent. Tell him how it works."

Luc sat back in his chair and crossed his arms. "Criminals don't care about the deals they make with idiots. Well, they care about how they can use you. And how they can please the next guy up the chain, so they don't get a bullet in the back of their head. They sell off loans, they sell off favors, and if the right person asks, they aren't paid in money; they trade favors or second chances."

"So how did it start?" Gena asked. "Who asked for the

first favor? They'll be low on the ladder. You won't know anything to help us arrest the head of the organization, but we'll work our way up to the guy we want."

"I need a break," Dean said. "You have to give me a break if I ask for one." He turned to me. "You're a witness. I asked them to leave me alone."

"You need water?" Luc asked as they stood. "Low blood sugar? The bathroom?"

"Can she stay?" Dean asked. "Yes, some water. I just need to think."

"We'll give you fifteen minutes," Gena said. "She comes with us. You haven't earned any concessions."

He dropped his head on his arms without saying anything.

"He's almost ready," Andy said as we headed into the observation room. "Good work."

Gena tossed the file on the table and grabbed a bottle of water. "He still might ask for a lawyer. I suggest Charity take a more supportive role."

If they thought it would work, I'd give it a try. "I'll move my chair closer to him. Not within reach, maybe just around the edge of the table. What do you think he's doing?"

A constable entered the interview room and handed Dean an opened water bottle. He asked Dean if he felt okay. Dean nodded and took a drink. The constable reminded him that if he needed one, they had a doctor on duty. I noticed he didn't remind him he was entitled to call a lawyer.

"That should soften him a bit," Luc said. "If we're right, Charity, he's thinking about what he's going to tell us. Weighing the value of each bit of information."

Gena finished her water and put the bottle in the recycle bin. "Are we ready to go back in?"

"It's only been five minutes," I said, checking the time.

"He doesn't have a great sense of time now he's been in the room a while," David said. "We are obligated to give him a break, but five minutes is enough."

There was a whole world of hurt in these techniques. If I never got involved with one again, I'd be happy. I squeezed David's shoulder as we made our way back into the room, then dragged my chair around the corner of the table and sat.

"Are you feeling ready to talk?" I asked in an effort to seem to be on his side.

His skin had gone pale, and a sheen of sweat had formed at his temples. "Who are you trying to get?" he asked. "I mean, the head of the organization. There are a few, and maybe I'm not connected to the right gang. What happens if I can't help you arrest your big fish?"

"Don't worry about that," Gena said. "We're happy to take down all kinds of scum. We just want someone bigger than you."

He hesitated.

"How will this work out?" I asked for his benefit. "I mean, he's been here a long time. If they think he's helping us, then he needs protection, right?" I reached over and patted his arm. Maybe the touch sent my act overboard, but we hadn't taken the time to discuss how I would get him on side.

"We'll send him back to work," Luc said. "We'll make some official statement that he was unable to help our inquiries. We'll also find a way to put the word out that maybe he's not bright enough to know anything. Will that be enough?"

I looked at Dean.

He looked like he was going to argue about being

painted as stupid, but his shoulders dropped, and he took a long inhale. "Yeah. I don't think they know how much I figured out. So, it should work."

Unless Kuznetsov didn't want to take a chance that he would talk and might know something.

"Start talking," Gena said.

"I gave some information to a prisoner. A couple of years back. His lawyer used it to get him off a nothing charge. I got a grand. Then we had an arrangement with the lawyer."

"Name?"

Dean cleared his throat. "Gregor Popov."

"Is that your only contact?"

"I can probably come up with a list of criminals I helped. I didn't exactly keep records. But there is one more thing."

We all looked at him while he swallowed and seemed to struggle to find the words.

"You have to tell us," I said. "We can't help you if we don't know everything you know."

"Okay, so this is just something I overheard. I got outside early for that killer. I heard her on the phone before she noticed me. She was speaking some kind of Eastern European language, maybe Russian, maybe Ukrainian."

"What did she say?" Gena asked. "A name? What kind of tone?"

"No. I don't speak any other languages, but I kind of recognized the sounds. Maybe she was arguing, but maybe just checking in."

Gena slapped the file closed on her final notes. "Okay. We'll end the interview now and see if this is enough to earn you your deal."

21

W e left Dean in the interview room and joined David and Andy in the observation space. It was too small for all five people to sit, and I hoped we'd be out in a few minutes.

I don't know what they got out of his final answers, but I was ready to follow up on a tattoo database, or on the Russian connection. It wouldn't be Kuznetsov, nothing worked out that easy. Whoever this woman was talking to, though, was a link in the chain. Now I needed to get the official take on it, and maybe give mine.

"What happens to him next?" I asked. "You let him go?"

"Not yet," Andy said. "We have a few hours leeway before our story about him being useless loses credibility."

A sound from next door drew my attention to the one-way glass. A couple of constables were taking Dean out while he protested.

"So, what are the initial impressions?" Andy asked.

Gena relaxed against a wall. "We'll need to verify with the recording, but I think we got everything he knows. You saw when he gave up trying to win the game."

"He isn't a part of the gang," Luc said. "We never thought his information would get us far, but we can see what calls went through the local towers, maybe we'll be lucky."

"How many Russian gangsters are there in town?" I couldn't pull dumps from cell towers, so I had no idea what the odds were.

"You mean outside Kuznetsov's gang?" David asked. "No idea. Only a few gangs have racial restrictions. Basically, if you can bring in an income stream, you're in. If that dries up and you can't replace it, then you're out, sometimes permanently."

"But not Kuznetsov's, right?" Gena said. "We can't shop for clues, but Kuznetsov's inner circle is likely Russian."

"What does that mean?" My experience of his gang was that people who failed him, and didn't hide well, turned up dead. "They can screw up and survive?"

"No. They are vicious. And you don't need to be the one who screwed up to die. If anyone you're connected to screws up, you die."

So, Viktor died because Alan screwed up? I needed to find Cynthia before we found her body. "Is there a database of assassins?" I asked. "I mean, their methods, any identifying marks, known associations?"

"Yes. It's not just local either. The FBI, Mossad, everyone puts in whatever data they gather. Even forces we can't fully trust have access. Interpol manages it."

The way she said it made it sound like a questionable benefit. I hoped it was just a touch of territorial snobbery and not an indication that the controls were too loose to trust the information. "What else did you learn from Dean's confession?"

"We'll take another go at him," Gena said. "I'm pretty sure that's all he knows, but maybe he can try to give us something from what he overheard that we can translate. You want in on that?"

No. I had things to do. I'd tell them about Viktor's wife once I had a little traction — or when I ran into a wall I couldn't bash though. I couldn't rely on them keeping me on the team, so I needed my own clues. "If he won't talk without me there," I said. "But I'd rather not."

"And what did you think of the interview?" Gena asked.

"That you do a good badass," I said with a laugh. "One day I'd love to learn how you do that."

"You planning on conducting interviews?" David asked.

I hoped never to sit and watch someone break like that again. I got the feeling Dean was easy, but the moment when I told him he had to help us, I saw something die in his eyes. "It would be nice to learn how to act a character if I need to go undercover on an insurance fraud case."

"Your take on the results?" Andy asked.

"Okay. He has some names for you," I said. "I'd follow up on those. He gave you Gregor Popov's name. You can tell if he's a mob lawyer, right? I think it's Kuznetsov, or one of his inner circle, who ordered the hit, but you're right that the link is pretty tenuous."

"We should get out of here," Luc said. "I need some freshly conditioned air and room to think."

"Go start on the phone tower dump and the Interpol records," Andy said to Gena and Luc. "We'll join you in a few minutes."

I braced for the speech about how it was too dangerous for me to be on the case. Andy closed the door and gestured for me to sit. "What are you holding back?"

Crap, he was too good at this. "Same goes for you. What are you not saying? I mean, I get that you need to stick to the rules, but you don't tell me everything."

David took the seat next to me. "Charity, yes, there are things we need to hold close so if we manage to bring the case to court, the defense has little or nothing in the way of technicalities. Your being on the team is a big technicality in itself, but we've covered that with contracts. If you know something, you need to tell us."

"So you can throw me off the case?" I didn't like the feelings running through me. I was sappy because David was being kind and rational. I was mad because David was being kind and rational. Maybe working together was a lousy idea. "I don't know anything for sure. I have a few ideas."

Andy nodded and waited.

"Do you really want me to tell you and find yourself in one of those technical issue problems?" Just assuming, but if they didn't know what I was going to do, it wouldn't damage the case.

Andy sighed like he was dealing with a five-year-old looking for a loophole to stay up past bedtime. "Asking that question is already a technicality issue. We are capable of investigating a case, Charity."

"If Gena is right, then Viktor isn't the only one on this woman's hit list. When we took down Alan Blackhouse, there were a lot of associates left hanging out. We arrested the Guptas, and we had Victor McCarthy. But we don't know if the people smuggling the kids into Vancouver are in danger." Not that I cared if they showed up dead or went missing forever. I didn't care that much about Cynthia except she might be the connection to Kuznetsov.

Andy nodded at me, and I expected to be asked for a list of names, but he said, "Let's go see what Gena and Luc found so far. We can do another known associates search to see if we find other leads to follow."

22

I followed Andy and David to the case room not believing anyone bought my act. At the least, Andy should have made me tell him names. I couldn't get a handle on him. Every time I thought I had him pegged as someone who didn't want me on the team, and didn't trust civilians on principle, he gave me leeway. I got a sudden rush of empathy for the criminals he interrogated.

I expected to be dumped again without notice, so having a bit of investigative information of my own meant I could continue without supervision. Unless Guy stopped giving me tips, or I couldn't pull leads from any other sources.

For now, I was happy to learn everything the RCMP had — and contribute to the investigation, of course.

"What do we have so far?" Andy asked as we entered. Gena and Luc sat hunched over keyboards, and both screens displayed forms with all the fields completed.

Gena didn't look up from her screen as she waved toward the whiteboard. "We've got names on the board of some contract killers. And the tattoo? Kills. Each one is a contract fulfilled."

Like tears on gang members. "All of them do that?" I moved closer to the board to read the names.

"No. Mostly Russians, or some South Americans." Gena stood and wrote another assassin's name on the list.

"Are these all women?" I asked.

Andy joined me. "I doubt anyone knows. These names are gathered from anecdotes, I think. None of them will turn out to be on any birth certificates." He turned to Luc and Gena. "Any MOs?"

David was reading Luc's screen over his shoulder. "It looks like some, but nothing proven. No one's been arrested, so we can't rely on the method of killing to lead us to the killer."

I read the names on the board. "Viper, Black Death, No Mercy, Stiletto, Eagle, Wraith. A bit dramatic."

"It's a branding thing," Luc said. "Who would hire a killer named Fluffy?"

The names still seemed over the top to me, but I wasn't in the market for a hitperson.

Gena grabbed a handful of papers from beside her keyboard and headed over to join me at the whiteboard. "There will be more people eventually, but this list is methods and I'll link them to the suspected killer."

She wrote strangulation, gunshot, stabbing, poisoning, sniper shot, garroting, staged suicide, car crash, then drew lines with a different color to each name. It might not be reliable, but there was definitely a vague pattern. Two of them were capable of sniper shots, which I'd always thought was a specialist skill someone learned in the armed forces. One of them didn't poison anyone, two didn't stage suicides or accidents.

"Does this help?" I asked.

"A bit," David said. "In this many cases, we can be confident that this Viper doesn't use poison, and Stiletto doesn't fake accidents or suicides. But we could be looking at too small a list to make a good correlation."

I stared at the board. Dean's picture was there, along with Viktor's. Kuznetsov's was at the top, but no lines connected him to any point or picture. The list of killers and methods was the only other information. I closed my eyes and took a deep breath before opening them again and blurring my gaze. I needed a new perspective on the information, and this had worked in the past.

What was missing? Cynthia's name. The links between Viktor and Kuznetsov. There were no known associates for any of the pictures. We had nothing as far as I could tell.

"What about people connected to Dean? Or to Viktor?" I still wasn't ready to hand over Cynthia's name if they didn't already have it.

"You think Dean's buddies are in danger?" David asked. "We can't keep our eyes on everyone."

"The lawyer?" I pointed out. "His name isn't on the list."

"We're still doing some background," Gena said. "He'll go up if we find anything shady."

Like he hired the hitperson?

"Any family members?" I asked. "They could be used against Dean."

"No spouse, no kids, parents dead, only sister lives in Miami." Luc rattled off the details. "We don't want to clutter the board, but that doesn't mean we aren't gathering intel."

"Sorry," I said. "We tried to put everything up in my previous murder investigation. It helped."

David turned on his laptop. "Different ways of doing the same thing, Luc. It's not Charity's fault she doesn't know

Andy's process. I'll look into Popov's list of cases. It will help to see if there's a pattern of him working for Kuznetsov or one of his lieutenants. We don't want to go after him if our evidence is sketchy."

"Can I get access?" I asked. "It's hard for me to help out when we're sorting through records. If I can't do my own research."

"No," Andy said. "No civilians in our databases."

Time for me to head out. "Okay, I'll see you tomorrow." I'd pick up some takeout and start the search for Cynthia.

"Good idea," Andy said. "We'll probably have something to follow up on in the morning."

His phone rang as I pulled my stuff together.

"Is he dead?"

Andy's question stopped all the movement in the room.

"We'll leave him until tomorrow. Any details on who did it?"

He ended the call without asking anything else.

"Dean Marshall was attacked. He survived and is in St. Paul's, but the doctor put him under sedation until tomorrow. We stationed a guard on his door. I'll send someone we can trust to take over security."

"Details?" I asked. The caller had said a fair amount before Andy hung up.

"A woman got in the room somehow and stuck a knife in his side. Missed anything major, but he fell from the chair and smacked his head on the floor before anyone found him. Concussion."

"How did the killer get back in?" Gena asked before I could sort out a coherent question from my racing thoughts.

"Under investigation. Gena, go down and make sure they find out. I want competence, not more corrupt stupidity."

"Do contract killers fail?" I asked.

"The first attempt isn't always successful," Luc said. "The contract isn't over until the target is dead."

23

I
f the killer planned on trying until Dean was dead, then we had an opportunity. I couldn't set a trap without Andy's help or asking David to violate his rules. It wasn't just access; it was authority I needed.

"When she tries again, we can be waiting." I wasn't going to start out by saying I would be springing the trap. Best to avoid starting our plan on an argument.

"That's the plan," Andy said. "You can observe from here. We'll make sure cameras are working. Having a record will be an asset in court."

No way was I staying so far away from the action. "Why here? I could watch from that room in the jail."

"This is Gena and Luc's case," David said. "You are on our team, not theirs. Andy and I will be here too."

Oh, that gave me a new angle. Gena and Luc seemed more open to me contributing during the interview, so maybe I wouldn't need to fight too hard to get in on the arrest.

"What's the plan?" I asked Gena. "Maybe I have some ideas to help."

Gena looked up from her screen that was now split into six windows, each displaying a different view. Five were of corridors in a hospital, and one of Dean in his bed. "We wait for her to act. We position someone to grab her when she goes in to finish the job."

Just wait? What if the killer took days to prepare? I mean, did she think we would let her march in and shoot Dean without someone noticing? "Can we try to force her hand?"

"That can go wrong," Andy said. "If she thinks we're luring her, she'll stop until it's safe. We can't keep up this surveillance level for more than a few days. We're counting on Kuznetsov, or whoever put out the contract, to be impatient. The longer Marshall is in our custody, the more likely he is to talk."

I should have known they considered rushing the killer. It would increase the chances she'd make a mistake, after all. "What if I can think of a way to push her that seems natural?"

"Like pretending he needs to be moved today?" Luc said with a sigh. "Or, having Crown Counsel visit like he's getting protection?"

"Charity is imaginative," David said. "If she has an idea, you should at least listen. It's not like our usual ideas are going to work against someone like this killer. You need to think that if Kuznetsov put out the contract, the penalty for failure is going to be a slow, painful, and messy death, right?"

I hadn't given any thought to what happens in the case of failure. "Is that what failing to fulfill a contract usually means?"

"It doesn't happen often enough for there to be a usual outcome. No one gets into that business without skills and history. A few have been found dead. I guess a contract gets taken out on them. David's right. If this is Kuznetsov, he'd want to take care of it personally."

The trickle of satisfaction at the idea of this woman being treated to torture and death was outweighed by the fact that it made me sick. And it made me wonder if that was the plan. Stop her from fulfilling the contract. Then somehow track her to Kuznetsov and catch him in the act. I couldn't bring myself to ask the question because a yes meant David agreed to it, and I didn't think he was that kind of man.

"How will she know when it's time to try again?" I asked instead as an idea formed to catch her now before Kuznetsov got a chance.

"Probably bribing someone on staff at St. Paul's," Gena said. "Why?"

The idea wasn't complete, but I had enough to start. "What if I went in and sat with him? He did trust me, so it might not be too hard to convince him to let me stay. We want to keep the cover in place that he's got nothing to trade for a deal."

"No."

All four voices at the same time. Seemed like a bit of overkill. Well, I was an expert at ignoring that word.

"Give me a chance here. As I go in, we are vocal about how awful it is that a guard would be attacked for no reason. That we should have released him right away and dealt with the paperwork later. That we need to apologize."

"We don't apologize," Gena said. "Makes it hard to deny culpability if someone sues."

"That's cold." I understood the rationale, but if they screwed up, they were culpable. They did deal with criminals, so maybe I only had half the story. Something to ask David when we were alone.

"In this case, Dean's guilty, so we can't say sorry," Andy said.

He didn't shut me down, so I continued, "We can figure out the finer details later. The important thing is that whoever is on the killer's payroll needs to hear us so it seems normal that a friend will sit with him until he's moved."

"He's in St. Paul's. Where would we move him?" Gena asked.

"It's not about the quality of the medical care," I said. "I mean, think about it. If he was innocent, wouldn't you be moving him to a more secure location? One you control." I counted on the fact that the RCMP had a place to keep injured people they wanted protected.

The four of them exchanged glances. Time to stop selling my idea and let them agree, or even make it their idea. I had to save my arguments for making sure I was the one in that room.

"It could work," Gena said. "She's got a point that we've been thinking of Marshall as a criminal when we want the world to think of him as innocent."

"It's too dangerous for Charity to go in," Andy said. "David, you agree it should be one of us, right?"

"Sorry, Inspector," Gena said, "as you pointed out, this is our case. I think she's exactly the right person. We'll make sure she's safe."

24

I expected Andy to pull rank on Gena about the trap, and he did seem to be fighting an internal argument, but he agreed and let us plan the details.

Which resulted in me sitting beside Dean's bed in St. Paul's with a guard outside, named Phillipe, who'd been ordered to look less than useful. So, he flirted with the nurses and any patients wandering the halls. It was a restricted access ward, so no visitors to complicate things.

The scene was set for our mystery killer to walk in and find out that Dean had company, if she hadn't been warned about me. I was wired to the guy outside. I had a safety word. Gena said it wasn't called that, but I didn't care.

If I said 'memorable', Phillipe would rush in and capture our killer. And then we'd break her, and then we'd arrest Ivan Kuznetsov, and the world would be a safer place. Until the next psycho took over the gang. Not the most exciting of traps, but Gena said simple was less likely to fail.

"They should've moved me," Dean mumbled. "This is dangerous."

I had to maintain my cover of being his friend so he

wouldn't kick me out. He'd been acting all entitled to special treatment since the attack. Like he suddenly believed he was innocent, and it was our fault he'd been there for someone to attack him.

"How could we do that without the killer seeing it?" I asked.

The door opened and a nurse came in. Not our hitwoman in disguise. Unless she was able to pass as a twenty something Malaysian guy, we were safe. He checked the machines, asked if Dean was comfortable, nodded to me and left.

I had a printout of the best image we had of the killer as a lawyer. We expected the new disguise to be nurse, food delivery, or some other hospital staff. Dean wasn't that badly hurt. Unlikely to need physio or occupational therapy, so no specialists popping in to talk. His wound was clean and dressed. He'd be released back to jail or whatever tomorrow after observation because of his head injury.

"I was thinking of you," Dean said. "Dangerous for you."

I didn't believe it. How would moving him be safer for me? I opened my mouth to ask but the fire alarm went off. I sniffed the air but didn't smell smoke. My first thought was for all the oxygen. Were we going to blow up?

Dean struggled with his blankets, trying to unwrap himself. I knew he couldn't just leave. I looked at the closed door. Evacuation instructions. I ran over to read it and only just avoided being smashed in the nose as Phillipe pushed it from the other side. "Get ready. We're going together."

I pointed to the instructions on the door. "It says to wait."

"No. We have our own plan." He glanced at Dean, who'd finally unwound the cocoon of bed linen. "This could be the hitwoman. If we follow those rules, we'll play into her hands. Unpredictable is safer."

Dean got himself up. I handed him a second robe to wear back to front to cover his ass.

"You stay in the middle," I said. "Don't do anything stupid."

He grabbed his side like the wound hurt but just nodded instead of grumbling.

Outside the room no one was panicking. The halls were busy with people all headed in the same direction — out.

"Stay as close as possible," Phillipe said as he led us toward the stairs. "Let me know if I'm going too fast."

"You already are," Dean grunted the words.

I gave him a gentle prod. "We can go slow enough for her to kill you, if you like."

He hissed like I'd jabbed his wound; it was on the other side of his body, so not possible. "Fine. I can go a bit faster."

We'd reached the stairwell during this delightful conversation. Phillipe shouldered the door open and peeked inside, pulling back fast. "Clear." We followed him down the five flights to the street level.

The lobby was busier. The various offices and gift shop were closed, but still a steady stream of people headed out to the street. There wasn't a lot of room to gather outside on Burrard or Comox Streets, so the emergency wardens ushered people to gathering points farther away. We wouldn't have a handy crowd to hide in when we exited. "When we get outside, won't we be easier to attack?"

Phillipe drew us aside out of the flow of people. "We wait here until Andy sends the signal. Transport will be waiting when we leave."

I looked around at the crowd. If the killer was here, then this was the best chance to take Dean out. If she stuck to the same method, I expected her to be looking for an opening to stick a knife in Dean, and maybe me and Phillipe if she got lucky.

"Do we know if the alarm is legitimate?" I asked.

Phillipe spoke into a mic on his shoulder. Asking whoever was watching from outside. "Not yet. They found the location: an empty OR."

I kept scanning the evacuees. One woman caught my attention. Around the right build, red hair, blue scrubs. I knew the color of the scrubs meant something, but I had no idea what. She was talking to an old lady struggling with a walker. What bothered me was the way she glanced around. Looking for her target?

"See her?" I asked Phillipe.

"Yes. We can't go after her, Charity." Phillipe spoke into the mic again, reporting on the sighting. "Someone will be waiting for them."

I stopped scanning and focused on the aide. She got the old woman walking again and escorted her to the door. No longer looking behind at us, or whatever held her attention earlier.

They reached the doors and I saw a constable approach. The young woman gestured to the older one as if saying she needed to help her out. The old woman kept walking away, like she had someplace to be.

"Short in the circuit," Phillipe said. "No fire, we can go back."

"We've lost her," I said as I watched the old lady ditch the walker and hurry through the pedestrians.

25

The woman was gone by the time I made it to the street. Two RCMP officers ran back to join Andy, who stood beside a black SUV while David leaned inside to talk on the radio.

"Out of sight before we got to the intersection," the first officer to return said. "Too many people on the street, too easy to get lost in the crowd."

The young woman was talking to another uniformed officer, and the walker now carried a tag with an evidence number and date.

David put the mic on its stand and joined us. "Phillipe and Dean are back in the room."

"I don't think she had anything to do with it," I said.

"What? The young lady over there?" Andy cocked his head in the direction of the interview going on a few feet away.

"No, I meant the killer. If she'd caused the alarm, I would expect her to be doing something other than evacuating. The girl? Maybe she was just doing the old lady a favor. But if we interview her, we might get a better description."

As I watched, the officer handed a card to the girl. She pocketed it and then hurried back through the hospital doors. The officer joined us after checking his notes.

"She's a volunteer. Saw the old lady struggling and helped her out." He gave the report in a monotone.

"Any new details for the description?" Andy asked.

"Pretty good disguise. She noticed colored contacts made her eyes green. Wondered why an old lady would bother trying to look better. Now we've told her it was a disguise, she says the killer knew exactly how to pretend to be ancient. And she thought the woman was wearing colored contacts because old people usually have faded out eyes."

Andy checked something on his phone and told the officer to give his full report to Gena. "Fire inspector says no interference with the wiring. One of the reasons they're moving St. Paul's to a new building, too many old wires trying to do work beyond their capabilities. Okay, next steps?"

"We need to release Marshall with the story intact. Maybe he'll drop off her radar," David said. Then after looking at the expression on my face, he added, "We'll keep him protected until it's clear she's not coming back, or we catch her and lock her up. But he doesn't know enough to earn protection with a deal, and we agreed not to arrest him if he cooperated."

If he wasn't such an annoying pain in the ass, maybe someone would find a way to give him a better deal. "Maybe we should have an officer undercover? If she makes another attempt, we might catch her."

"That's always the plan, Charity." Andy checked his phone again. A text I couldn't read upside down. "We've got more leads to check up on. Popov only defends organized crime clients. So, he's a possibility. We'll follow up on the information we got from the database. If she's adding beads to her tattoo, we might get lucky with the artist."

"Is the lawyer on the *suspicious and needs to be interviewed* list?" Andy's comment didn't sound like it. I wasn't volunteering but if they were afraid to interview a lawyer, we might never catch Kuznetsov.

"Yes," David said. "We need more evidence than he has shady clients. Everyone gets a lawyer, and if he's crooked, he'll hide behind every trick to keep us from learning the truth."

So, low on the list for now. It felt like we were back at square one, or maybe even square zero. Just because the trap failed, didn't mean it was over. This killer wouldn't give up. And she was the closest we would get to Kuznetsov. If he placed the contract, that is.

"Do I go back to the room?" I didn't want to sit with Dean until the doctor released him. Phillipe could protect him without my assistance, and even if I turned out to be right about the killer trying again, she wouldn't risk another attempt in the hospital now that we'd come so close to catching her. People were too alert after the evacuation. Too ready for the next disaster.

David opened the door to the SUV for me. "No, come back to the office. Gena will want to debrief you."

Being in the back seat alone made me feel like a criminal. I tested the door handle before I did up my seatbelt in case this was a prisoner transport vehicle with disabled locks. I'd walk or take a cab if I couldn't leave when the car moved. The door popped open. I slammed it closed and clicked the seatbelt shut.

"How much more can we expect from the full interview?" I asked.

"All the impressions from the witness. What they talked about while she was escorting our killer. How she persuaded the old woman to accept help — old people can be difficult if they feel patronized. It will solidify the picture we're forming about her."

David's phone pinged. Texts seemed to be the preferred communication for cops as well as teenagers.

"Shit," he said. "Gena said the killer identified Marshall's escorts."

That meant me. "Identified? As in our names?"

"She asked the volunteer why a policeman stood there waiting while people were in danger."

I was standing with Dean and Phillipe. Maybe she thought I was only some visitor waiting for a chance to leave? "And?" I asked. "Am I about to be protected off the case?"

"We'll talk about it at the office," Andy said. "For now, you stick with us."

The traffic was its normal stop-and-go nightmare as we crossed downtown to get to the office. The silence in the car felt so unnatural, I wished I'd decided to walk instead.

"I need coffee," I said when Andy parked. "Not that crap in the break room." I wanted to avoid being shut in his office arguing that I didn't need to be locked up for safety.

"You can't go alone," Andy said.

"I'll do a coffee run while you go in," David said.

I followed Andy into the elevator and waited with him until we arrived on the right floor.

"Cheer up. You aren't going to the electric chair," Andy said. "We don't have one."

My phone buzzed in my pocket. A text from Guy. I glanced at it as I walked behind Andy.

Kuznetsov knows who you are.

Great. Now I'd probably have a contract on my own head. And my own little protective prison.

Andy left me in his office to check on Gena and Luc's whereabouts. No way could I make it out of the building before he noticed.

I sent a text back.

How bad?

He responded immediately. *Not terminal yet from what I overheard. Stay low profile. I'll get more details.*

I sent him a thumbs up emoji.

26

D avid showed up with coffee and cookies before Andy joined me again. I had no doubt what was coming. It would be considered gross negligence if they let me investigate knowing I'd come to the attention of a killer. It's not like I have some kind of death wish, but I do not sit by safely while people I love charge into danger. They didn't worry about Phillipe's safety, and he'd been there beside me when the woman noticed us.

Okay, he had a gun, and training, and backup. But if I hadn't been willing to take a big risk, Alan Blackhouse would still be laundering money, Glenda might be dead, and Nora might just be another statistic of child pornography.

Andy grabbed his coffee, then peeked into the bag of cookies. "Nope, I won't."

He had more self-control than I did. I grabbed the one I'd designated in my mind as his and took a bite. Peanuts, salt, and butter. Heaven.

"We've got a name from the description the volunteer gave," Andy said. "The killer uses the name Viper. She's been in business about six years, pretty long for that profession. She works for a variety of organizations, so we can't tie her to Kuznetsov unless she tells us he hired her."

That was progress. "So, why are we in your office and not with Gena and Luc?" I wanted action, and this felt like so many steps back. We weren't even sitting and watching someone analyzing data.

"They need focus," David said. "A couple more officers joined the team. Too many voices making suggestions, too many eyes."

"So, what are we going to do?" I asked. Andy's office was too awkward for three of us to work in. The concrete pole made it impossible to sit together without being oddly close. It did seem weird that someone with Andy's rank would be assigned such an uncomfortable place to work. "Who did you piss off to get this office?"

"I don't spend a lot of time in here, so I don't much care about it," Andy said. "Before we go anywhere, you need to tell me what you're holding back."

I looked at David, not sure why I thought that would help. When I marshalled my argument to stay on the team, I didn't even consider he'd guess I was holding back again. My poker face needed work.

David didn't rush to my rescue, so he'd guessed too.

"It's nothing," I said. "You know all about the dangers. You know this Viper asked about me."

Andy shook his head at me. "That's not all. You've been quiet — for you — since you got that text."

For one second, I thought he'd ask to see my phone. But both of them just waited and watched me.

"I don't want to be stuck in here while you catch Kuznetsov. I've put too much into the investigation."

"Spit it out," David said. "We can't work the case without all the information."

"Are you asking Phillipe these questions?"

"He's not hiding something," Andy said, exasperated. "If you know something, you need to tell us. We're a team. We need to trust each other."

That was a low blow. "If I tell you everything, you'll want the name of my source. I'm not doing that."

"Fair enough," Andy said. "But I also don't want to have this conversation again. Why don't you just tell us? Why is it always a struggle?"

I'd planned to tell them about the text — maybe not so soon though, and just the content, not the context. The trust issues discussion caught me off guard. The more rational side of my mind said I had no choice. If I don't trust them, I can't expect them to trust me. The paranoid side kept yelling that they would kick me off the team to protect me.

I decided to try being rational. "I think you'll kick me off the case or put me in protection if I tell you everything."

Andy went to say something, but David held up his hand. "She's right. You kicked her off the case before with less justification."

It took a long moment before Andy worked out what he could say. I pressed my lips together to keep from blurting accusations.

"Okay. Look, I can't promise you won't be shut down at some point. I can promise that it won't come from me. If I could give you a weapon and train you to use it, I would, but that's not an option. I'm going to rely on your history of getting out of the dangerous situations you leap into. One condition."

This was far better than I imagined. He didn't have to say

anything like that to convince me to share my information. "What condition?"

"You try not to leave us in the dark."

He wasn't the only one who couldn't promise things. "I can try, but no guarantees. If I see a situation where I need to act, I'm not going to wait for permission."

"Okay, that will have to do. What did the text say?"

I told him. "But he's known about me since the Alan Blackhouse case. You thought he was the guy in the night-club, remember? I'm in the same danger as I've been in all along."

They paused like they expected me to run out of steam before they lost patience. Then Andy asked, "Nothing else?"

I didn't need to tell him about my discussion with Gabe on the subject of contract killers, it was old news. "Yes. Now what are we going to do next?"

"Popov," David said. "We're going to talk to him."

"All three of us?" That seemed like overkill.

"Just you and me," David said. "He's our best lead left. We need to tread carefully, but we can't ignore our gut feeling that he's Kuznetsov's lawyer. First, we need to find another way to get this Viper in custody."

27

My phone buzzed. Unknown number. I hit ignore. If it wasn't spam, the caller could leave a voicemail. "How do you plan to contact her?" I asked. If we had another trap in mind, I figured it didn't include using Dean Marshall as bait.

My phone buzzed again. No voicemail, same unknown number. I hit ignore.

"How many people on her hit list?" David asked. "Not only Marshall. He's a clean-up from the original contract. But she has to eliminate witnesses, right?"

My phone buzzed again with a call from the same unknown. I accepted and snapped, "What?"

"Charity?" Dean Marshall asked.

"You called me, right? So, who else would it be?" I had no time for his bullshit. He was sitting in a nice safe hospital room with a guard. How urgently did he need to bother me?

I mouthed his name at David and Andy.

"She's coming to kill me," he said.

"Let me talk to Phillipe."

"He's not here. The nurse made him wait outside."

That didn't sound right. "Why would your guard leave you?" I looked at Andy when I asked the question. He nodded. I put the phone on speaker so I wouldn't need to keep repeating his side of the conversation.

"I don't know. I'm not a nurse. Something about giving me privacy. She told me I should be careful who I trusted. She said someone would come to deal with me."

I heard Andy talking to someone about getting back into the room, so I hit the speaker icon again. Too much noise and I didn't need Marshall hearing the plan.

"How are you calling me?" Part of me thought this was attention seeking. He didn't like being sidelined. The part of me that knew Viper was out to kill him couldn't take the chance he made the entire unlikely story up.

"The nurse left me a burner. I looked up your website. If you don't want people calling you, take the number off the contact info."

Andy left the room and David called someone. I figured my role was to keep Dean on the call long enough for them to sort out the problem.

"Did the nurse say anything else?" I hit the speaker as David ended his call.

"No. I guess she didn't need to make things specific."

"What did the nurse look like?" David asked.

"She looked like a nurse. They all look the same in those scrubs."

"How long ago did she leave?" I asked. I mean, he wouldn't be making this call with the woman who threatened him in the room, right?

"I called as soon as she left," Marshall said. "My security is still gone. That killer is probably coming in any minute."

David was back on another call.

None of this made sense to me. Why would Viper warn him? "We're looking for Phillipe," I said. "Stay on the call until someone comes."

"No. I'm leaving. You can't protect me." I heard a couple of grunts that made me think he was fighting the sheets again.

"You can't protect yourself either. We'll make sure you're safe."

"Like you've done up till now?" He whined and I had to grit my teeth to avoid calling him all kinds of names. I had one job. Keep him on the line until someone finds Phillipe.

"Who the fuck are you?" Dean snarled as I tried to think of another way to keep him from running.

Andy pulled open the door to his office, phone in hand. "Marshall, that is Constable Deauville. She will escort you to a secure location. Don't argue and don't delay."

"You're locking me up? We had a deal."

"Things have changed. It's for your own safety. No arrest, just protective custody."

He put his phone to his ear. "Deauville? You have permission to handcuff him if needed. Get him out of there fast." He ended his call, reached for my phone, and hit the red button.

"The team found Phillipe at the foot of the stairs. He's dead," Andy said as he sat behind his desk.

"How?" David asked.

I was too busy trying to wrap my head around the news to think of a question.

"We'll find out more when the medical examiner is finished, but it looks like a fight ending with a garroting, and the body pushed down the stairs."

120

P A WILSON

"Why would Viper warn Dean?" I asked. "Then kill Phillipe? Why not kill Dean?"

"We'll be sure to ask her," Andy said. "At a guess, she's sending us a message about no one being safe. I'll have the tech team look at Marshall's burner phone. Maybe our answers are there."

"But now we need to catch her," I said. "Right? Until she's locked up, no one is safe?"

David ended his call. "Nothing on the security cameras we set on the ward. No one on duty entered Marshall's room. No one noticed a new face, but the head nurse said they relied on us to vet anyone who had access."

Andy grabbed the last cookie and took a bite. "Gena will assign someone to review the entire footage for the hospital, but I guess we know it must be Viper. Unless Phillipe has someone in his personal life who'd kill him."

So, we were dealing with someone who knew how to avoid cameras that we'd put up in secret. She killed a cop, which I thought was off limits, but maybe that only happened on TV. "What now?"

"A trap. We leave Phillipe's murder to Gena, Luc, and CRCC."

"Who?" I'd managed to keep up with most of the jargon, but not that.

"Like internal affairs," David said. "Killed in the line of duty. Someone has to dole out the blame."

I let it go. Just another reason to work alone in the future. When things went wrong, no one else took the blame, or pointed a finger. "You have a plan? For the trap?"

Andy looked at David like he expected objections. "I think this was Viper looking for who Marshall would call in an emergency. If I'm right, she knows about you. More than seeing you in the hospital."

"I'm not going into protective custody."

David's face flushed with anger. He spoke, choosing his words like he had to stifle a profanity before each one, "He means you to be the bait, Charity. I hate the idea, but he's right. We'll make sure you're safe. She won't get near you."

28

I n the end we had a pretty simple plan. Make sure I was seen out and about to get her attention. Then, when she tried to kill me, grab her. I had to admit a big part of me wanted to run and find a deep, dark cave to hide in. If I was walking around, how would my backup protect me? And the rest of me bubbled with excitement. I liked the excited part best.

David still seethed every time I looked at him. And he spoke in monosyllables when he said anything. I figured he didn't want to say enough to break some kind of dam and end up trying to put an end to the whole thing. I appreciated that he knew better than to try to stop me —and that he wanted to.

I had on my leather jacket to cover the bulk of the bullet- and stab-proof vest. We were relying on Viper sticking to her stabby approach rather than turning sniper.

The plan started with a fake argument in the parking lot that resulted in me storming off. If Viper didn't suspect a trap, it should look legit. If she was watching, that is.

I refused to head home because I had neighbors and

didn't want them to be collateral damage. Normal activity for me would be to try to find information from my sources. And I refused to involve them because no way would I be able to keep their identities out of it. So, a walk to a coffee shop for a latte, and then to a bench in Crab Park where I would look like a target but could be observed. And it ran along the water, so always a benefit for me. And not hugely popular in the evenings, so few bystanders.

I SAT, propped my laptop on my knees, and pretended to research. It was harder than I imagined to pretend to be interested in a fake Google search. I'd been told not to keep looking around because it would tip Viper off, so I only looked up when a kid laughed across the park, or a car honked its horn. The first time, I tried to be subtle about scanning the area for approaching hitwomen. The second time, I stopped myself before I scanned for cops.

You are not bait. You are searching for information. You are here for some innocent reason. I let the mantra run in my mind as I typed a search for a recipe into Google. I don't cook, but it was all I could think of.

I had an earpiece so Andy could talk to me. Not David, because he couldn't guarantee to keep himself under control. He was there though, watching me. I could talk back but I felt weird doing it. Like I was talking to myself. If I couldn't watch for Viper, I needed to rely on my watchers to alert me.

A kid laughed and I looked up. A woman walked my way. The right height and build, bit too far for me to recognize. Disguise could only take Viper so far, but she was medium everything, so that gave her a head start in the not-being-noticed game.

The woman kept coming. Not confirmation of a threat since I was sitting on the first bench inside the park with a street behind me. She walked with purpose. The path would pass in front of my bench.

No one spoke in my ear, but they must see her. I fought the urge to ask. The woman came too close to make that safe. Then she strode past me. Not Viper.

"Heads up," Andy's voice chirped.

I kept my eyes on my laptop. *I am working in the fresh air, too focused to see anyone coming.*

The plan counted on me being unaware of her as a threat. It didn't make a difference that I could hear kids laughing somewhere or catch snatches of conversations that came from so far away it should be impossible. The only people in the park with me were closer to the other side, almost two blocks away. The salty diesel scent from the water was turning my stomach even though it smelled the same at my home. I was on the verge of hyperventilation from trying to keep my breaths shallow.

The sound of footsteps behind me made me freeze. There was only so much I could do to override the urge to run. They passed. My shoulders relaxed, and I waited for Andy to give me the all clear.

"You shouldn't be sitting here alone." The woman's voice sounded light and cheerful despite the threat in the words. "Dangerous for a woman to be in such a place when it's almost dark."

I looked toward the sound like the intrusion offended my sense of privacy. It was her. She sat on the far end of my bench. Perched like a cat waiting to jump for prey. Her face was all angles without a disguise. She kept staring ahead, like in the movies when two spies meet on a park bench and hold a conversation without looking at each other.

Where was the cavalry? Did she have to attempt to kill me before they took her down?

"Same goes for you," I said.

She smiled, a thin, mean lifting of the corners of her lips. "Not everyone is as capable as me."

Was I supposed to pretend I didn't know her identity? Where the fuck was the cavalry?

"You sure I don't know how to take care of myself?" I didn't. If she reached over and stabbed me in the right place, I was dead. No Special Ops training, no Krav Maga.

"I'm pretty good at understanding what people are capable of," she said, still staring at the waves crawling up the sand as the tide came in.

Movement caught my eye behind Viper. Black clad, big gun. One of the protection team members but far back near the trees. Viper didn't move. It's not like she was trapped; the park didn't have a gate or fence. If she wanted to, she could just stand up and walk into the surrounding neighborhood. Viper was good at blending in. The cop couldn't just start shooting at her, because missing his target meant hitting something, or someone else. They'd need a more obvious threat.

Now I knew they had my back, I started to believe we would move closer to arresting Kuznetsov.

29

"Your friends are getting close," Viper said, still looking forward.

I really wanted to look around. The cavalry might be close by, but I couldn't figure out why they hadn't grabbed her by now. There was no point in pretending. "You don't seem worried."

She laughed. "They think I have a bomb."

That explained the caution, but not the fact that my earpiece remained silent. "And if I tell them you don't?"

"What makes you think they're wrong? I jammed your communications, by the way." She pulled her hand out of a pocket and showed me a small black remote, like a garage opener. "Why are you letting them put you at risk?"

I turned around to see if Andy or whoever waited to arrest her was in signaling distance. I didn't believe she would be willing to blow anything or anyone up. A bomb, even a small one, was overkill and didn't fit her reputation. I didn't much care why she sat here on my bench. I wanted her taken. The cop I'd seen creeping up earlier was gone. Probably hiding in the trees. I couldn't see anyone else.

I could yell bomb and hope she was bluffing, but if she wasn't and one person got injured, I'd never be able to forgive myself. And my job was to keep her here to give Andy or David a chance to catch her.

"You killed Viktor McCarthy and tried to kill Dean Marshall. Why wouldn't I take a chance if we get to put you away for a long time?"

I still had my laptop. More of a brick than a weapon, but maybe I could use it to bash her arm or head. I closed the lid to make the thing easier to swing.

"That was business. I don't do freebies, so you're safe unless someone is willing to pay me for your death. Viktor was a very bad man, so you should be happy." She shrugged and continued to look straight ahead.

Was I supposed to be grateful she took him out? Or did she really not care? I couldn't get a real grasp on her, and usually I was good at reading people. Maybe I just couldn't read sociopaths. "He worked for a worse one."

She pursed her lips with a little humph. I turned my attention back to the people ahead of us in the park. Everyone was packing up. I saw Luc walking toward a final group of young people and hoped they wouldn't argue just because they were teenagers.

"They are clearing the innocents, good idea." Viper turned to look at me. She was harder looking than I thought earlier. Her eyes were not exactly dead but didn't shine with any emotion I recognized. "Soon your friends will come for me. I will not be taken."

"You failed to fill your contract on Marshall," I said. "You might be safer in custody."

She tipped her head and smiled. "Kuznetsov can get to me anywhere. But you are right. I may choose to surrender to your police if I think Kuznetsov is tired of giving me chances. That man should have been dead the first time, or the second, but he seems to have the luck of the devil."

She was going to escape. The park was empty now. Only her, me, and whoever comprised the cavalry. "Sometimes assholes are lucky. I'm not telling you where he is."

"I know this already. I came to tell you that I will call if I am in need of your services. There is a phone beside me on the bench. I will use that number, do not call me. If anyone else picks up, I will not speak. I will, how do you say, go down in a blaze of glory?"

"What the fuck is that supposed to mean?" I'd run out of patience. If she wanted me as a lifeline, she needed to stop playing games. This cryptic bullshit was wasting my time.

"I will go after Kuznetsov and kill anyone in my way. I will die, sure, but maybe I will leave a message for anyone else thinking an assassin is expendable. And I will be a legend either way."

She stood and took a step onto the path.

"Why risk it?" I asked, turning to watch her. No one was in sight yet. They still thought she had a bomb.

She didn't answer me.

"No bomb!" I yelled toward where I thought Andy stood. "Grab her."

Three shadows slipped from behind trees. They raised their rifles.

Viper laughed and leaned down to push the burner phone toward me. I opened my mouth to tell her to stop. She sprayed something into my mouth. I swallowed automatically. Nothing burned or made me cough.

A garbage can exploded somewhere behind me.

30

"Are you hurt?" David checked my body before I could answer.

My thoughts were fuzzy. A reaction to the explosion? I let David inspect me for injuries. I didn't feel any pain, but shock can do weird things to you, and maybe I had a broken rib or a bleeding wound that I didn't register yet.

"She's not harmed," David said.

I looked up as Andy joined us. "Did you get her?" If this had all been for nothing, I was going to... I don't know what.

"No," Andy said. "She had us focused on you, and a potential explosion. By the time we got to the street she was nowhere in sight."

Either she had a car running all that time, or she hadn't left right away. Hiding behind a car would be pretty simple. It didn't matter because if she did hide to wait out the search, she'd be gone by now.

"Did you catch anything she said?" A headache started to throb at my temples.

"She jammed us," David said. "She knew exactly what we would do."

"I'll find out who gave her the intel to do that, and they'll end up paying for it," Andy said.

If the RCMP had a leak, we'd never catch Viper. Let alone Kuznetsov. I tried to think who would have enough information and wasn't on our list of most trusted. But my thoughts still fragmented like light through a prism. "Where was the bomb?" Maybe close enough for a concussion? The only thing I could think of to explain the fuzziness.

"Too far away to do any damage," Andy said. "She didn't intend to hurt anyone. Just a distraction."

I blinked and tried to focus my thoughts. Definitely something wrong because things were getting weird. I told David what was happening to me.

He turned my head to face him. "Did she touch you?"

"No." The spray? Something in it to muddle me? It didn't make sense that she would booby trap me if she wanted a lifeline. Had she lied about calling me?

I saw Andy waving to someone and tried to look, but I felt woozy. No, the trees were walking away, and I somehow thought that was a good idea.

Someone touched my hand. "What are you experiencing?" A woman's voice, sounding like a piano, all tinkly and in tune.

"The park is going blue," I said because no one else seemed to be noticing. "The trees are leaving, but more are replacing them — the new ones are rainbow striped. And there's a fairy sitting on your shoulder. Is she heavy?"

I didn't pay attention to the answer or any of the words around me because they were purple and tasted like banana.

"How about now?" the woman said again. This time I

looked at her. Normal woman. Blond hair tied back. Wearing ambulance attendant gear.

My hand hurt. "Less weird. What happened?"

"Did she give you anything?" David asked.

"Phone." I went to take it out of my pocket, but David grabbed my hand.

"She dosed you with something. Everything is fine. Let someone with gloves take the phone."

Dosed me? "I need it because she said she'd contact me." The park came into focus, no moving trees, no fairy.

"I think the drug must be salvia," the woman said. "Too fast for LSD, and it went within twenty minutes. Probably gone from your system now, but you need to get yourself checked out."

I was away for twenty minutes? "She sprayed me with something. I swallowed a bunch of it. I'm fine now, no need to go anywhere." I would not allow Andy to dump me in Emergency to wait for the all-clear while everyone else went looking for a mole or Viper.

The woman looked at David, who glanced at me with a frown but nodded.

"Fine. Look for signs of nervousness, irritability, or dizziness," she said. "Get her checked out today."

"We'll have our own doctor look at her," Andy said.

The woman left. A young constable snapped on latex gloves and asked for the phone. She took it from my pocket and promised to return it as fast as possible after they tested it for drugs, DNA, or fingerprints.

We were alone. Andy, David, and me sitting on a wooden bench in a park in the cold, waiting for the sun to set.

"Here's what will happen now," David said. "We'll take you back to the office, the on-call doctor will check you out.

If he gives the all-clear, you are back on the case. If not, you do what he recommends. Right?"

I figured if I argued, it would look like irritability and gain me a trip to hospital. And I did want to be sure I was fine. If Viper decided to call before they released the phone, I was pretty sure she'd try to reach me some other way because she would know the cops would want to check the phone even if she hadn't played games. I picked up my laptop. "Let's get on with it."

David sat with me in the back of Andy's car, like we were both under arrest, or teenagers on a date with dad. I giggled.

"What?" Andy said.

I shook my head. "Nothing."

My phone buzzed. I held it to my side so David wouldn't see the text. Not Viper, Guy.

New contract out on some chick named Viper.

I slid the phone back into my pocket. *I'll tell Andy and David when I get the all-clear from the nurse.* But I needed that burner back. Viper would hear pretty soon that she was a target.

31

I sat in my usual chair when we got back to Andy's office. He'd been called in to report to the boss, so we waited. I tossed my phone on the desk in case Guy texted.

No more hallucinations, but I wasn't my usual self either. Like I was waiting for the next monster to rise from the desk, or for Andy's face to bulge out.

"It's normal," David said as he sat beside me.

"Did I say something?" If I lost my ability to keep quiet, I was in big trouble.

"I can see it on your face. Waiting to find out if the trip is over, right?"

"Yes."

"You'll be fine soon. Just ignore the feeling of impending doom if you can."

Easy to say, but I guess knowing it was a side effect helped. "When will I get that phone back?"

"Not long. Andy told them to check for prints and DNA and return it to you ASAP in case she contacts you."

Guy's text made me think that would be sooner than

expected, or maybe her call would never come. If the new contract went to a better killer, or a sniper, then she would be dead before she tried to reach out.

"Why do you think she did it?" I struggled to make sense of the whole incident. "Dosed me, the bomb? Say she'd contact me? Or even come, when she guessed about the trap?"

"All good questions," Andy said, rejoining us. He tossed me the burner. "We'll ask her when we have her in custody. If you want me to guess, then I'd say she's well aware she screwed up and wants a safe out. You aren't a cop, so maybe you'd help."

"The bomb? The drug?" Why couldn't I think this through? More side effects?

"The explosion gave her space to leave." Andy sat behind his desk. "The salvia? What would you have done if she simply got up to leave?"

Of course, I would have gone after her. "It's a weird way to distract me."

Andy didn't answer.

I looked at David. "Figure it out. Using your brain will help you get past the effect."

His words made sense, but I didn't want to spend time trying to figure out the motives of a professional killer. "Shouldn't we be trying to find her?"

"The team is looking for front door cameras. Maybe one caught her getting into a car. Don't worry, we can take a moment. David, can you help the team?"

I watched as David left the room, then turned back to Andy. "What did Michel want from you?" I was stalling because if I couldn't figure out the reason Viper would do what she did, how would I continue to be a PI? And now David was gone, I didn't have an ally.

"We'll get to that." Andy moved his keyboard to the side.

"Okay, yes, she wanted to keep me on that bench. But if she wants me to be her safe out, she needs my trust. Dosing me isn't the best way to build trust."

"Could have been worse," Andy said. "She used a low dose of a non-addictive drug that would wear off soon even if we didn't have EMTs on site. It would have been as easy for her to inject you with a poison or a highly addictive drug."

I guess she could have shot me in the foot as easily too. "Fine. Your turn, Andy."

"He wants you to stay here in headquarters. He knows you can't be kicked off because you always find a way back on the team, but he thinks you'll sue if anything happens."

I couldn't be much help if I was stuck here. And just because they decided it was too hard to kick me out, didn't mean I couldn't choose to go. "And?" If he agreed with Benoit, I couldn't be any use on the team.

"I convinced him that you are our best lead to Viper. That we are fully able to protect you, and that you wouldn't take stupid risks. Was I wrong?"

The last part was the sticking point. Our definition of stupid might be completely different. "I am your best chance at catching Viper. I can act like a responsible adult."

Andy shrugged. "If you want to leave, we can find her without you."

I didn't want out. When she contacted me, I'd need the cops to back me up. But I also didn't want to keep hitting this barrier. "Why does he keep trying to kick me out?"

"He's under some kind of pressure. Maybe budget. We're expensive, and catching someone like Kuznetsov takes a long time. Or he doesn't like civilians. All I can be sure of is I can't continue fighting your side when you don't come clean about things you might know."

He kept all kinds of facts from me, so what made it worse when I protected my sources? "What do you think I'm hiding?"

He leaned toward me and pointed at my phone. "You received a message on the drive here. Are you telling me it has nothing to do with the case?"

How did he know it wasn't a friend? Or a client? Or spam? "I'm not handing you my sources."

"I'm not asking for names. Was the text related to our case?"

I couldn't lie. Andy may piss me off, but we both wanted Kuznetsov off the streets. "Someone put a contract out on Viper."

"Fuck, why didn't you say so immediately?" He reached for his phone. "We could be answering the request with an undercover operator."

I waited while he told someone to find the contract on Viper and close the deal. He slammed the headset down when he finished.

"This is a team, Charity. You can't withhold anything," he said.

Team only seemed to work one way. I was probably not supposed to make big decisions while the drug wore off, but I'd had enough of being used when they wanted something from me and shoved aside when they didn't. "How will you get to Viper without me?"

"We've put a tracer on the phone. She contacts you or you contact her, we'll know about it."

Good, they had a plan. "Will you read a text, or listen in on a conversation?"

"No."

"Is there a number in the contacts? Like she expects me to reach out even though she told me not to?"

"Numbers, but no real identities. She probably has multiple phones, and this way you'll get a caller ID. Why?"

I put the burner and my phone in my bag and stood. "I need some time away from all this." I didn't wait for his comment because I figured we'd actually be fighting if this went on long enough. I'd done my part in making sure I wasn't vital right now. I didn't quit the team. I didn't want to be kicked off. I just needed to be on my own.

I walked out of the building, checked around to see if I was being followed. Not as far as I could tell. And then got in my car, my stomach reminding me I should eat.

32

The first thing I did after ordering food in the restaurant was text David that I needed to take a break and not to worry. It wouldn't stop him reaching out to me, but I wasn't sure what Andy would say about me leaving.

Then I looked at the burner. I was pissed off at Viper for the prank — or distraction. I got that she needed a distraction and could have used any number of worse ones, but what she chose to do shook me up. I couldn't stop waiting for a hallucination to overtake reality. I trusted what David said about the anxiety being normal and a side effect, but knowing didn't stop the niggling fear that this was not reality. And it caught me by surprise, which made me afraid I was losing my touch and would never be able to solve a case again.

The waitress deposited my plate of bacon and eggs, topped up my coffee and left me alone. I went into the contacts on the burner and called the first of seven numbers, all with snake names as the ID. Andy was right. Any of them would be to Viper's phone.

The call rang out and no voicemail message came on. To be sure, I tried another four numbers; same thing, and my breakfast was getting cold. She'd know from the missed calls that I'd reached out. If she didn't call back, nothing I could do. I dropped the phone in my bag, slid toast under my eggs and started eating.

If this was my case, I'd be looking hard for Viper, but also following other clues. Cynthia Towers, Viktor's wife, was still on my list. I would check on any credit or debit cards in her name. Unlikely to help me move ahead of Ivan because he would have someone do the same. She'd be using an alias unless she was stupid, and I didn't get that vibe from her.

The contract on Viper might be underway, but I had no way of finding out who took it, or if a contract worked more like a bounty and whoever brought proof would get paid. I sent a text to Guy hoping he might know. I didn't want to be caught in the crossfire, but I did want Viper in custody. She was our closest contact to Kuznetsov.

David texted me. *Don't get killed. Come back soon.*

The three heart emojis made me smile. He could have phoned, but it's hard to argue on a text.

By the time I paid the bill, I had nothing more to follow up on. I needed a shower and a change of clothes. My laptop and phone needed charging, and I needed to find some background on Cynthia to help me find her and convince her to come in. Then I would go back to Andy, confident he wouldn't try to sideline me for a day or two. And I needed to crash soon, or I'd be imagining things from lack of sleep.

I STEPPED out of the shower and checked my phone. In the hour I'd managed to sleep, Guy had texted back a curt *no*. I didn't know if it meant no I'm not helping you, or no I don't know anything more, or no I can't talk now. While texts worked great when you didn't want to argue, they were crap for convincing people. And if Guy meant he couldn't talk, me responding might get him killed.

I dressed, put on a pot of coffee and pulled up my social media research on Cynthia from when I tried tracking Viktor down earlier. I knew her last name, Bashni in Russian, so did Kuznetsov. I tried to find a wedding certificate, but not knowing where they'd been married made that a long shot. If I had her maiden name, maybe I could find a lead. McCarthy wasn't a Russian name. I checked the arrest record, surprised I still had access, and I got two more aliases for Viktor: Volkov and Semenov, and his real last name: Morozov. Viktor Ilyich Morozov.

So many possibilities. I started searching for Cynthia with those last names in the male and female versions. Ivan might have all this information, but he didn't know that I did. I entered the Anglicized translations of all the names and waited. The program my hacker friend had created would search through multiple databases but my Wi-Fi speed would slow it down. She'd put a progress bar into the code, but in my experience, that was just a sop to me. The bar always got to fifty percent in seconds and then took forever before moving again, and then it always moved to one hundred percent. I watched it anyway.

Twenty minutes passed before I got a result, but I got six options. Victoria Bashni, Cynthia Semenov, Victoria Semenov, Cynthia Ilyich, Cynthia Volkov, and Victoria Morozov. At least one of them should be my target.

I started on the social media searches and eliminated four of the six by the profile pictures and posts, because fake profiles didn't usually come with family picnic or party images. Victoria Semenov and Cynthia Ilyich had no profile picture and were camera shy. It didn't matter because following up on two names was doable.

I looked for credit cards. Five cards between the two names. I followed up with my credit company contact and got transaction lists. That gave me a pattern and a starting point for surveillance. The case was moving forward, and I didn't need the RCMP or the cops to get a break. Okay, yes, I got the aliases from official databases, but the rest I did myself.

I found both aliases had a phone under their name. Not a burner, a regular phone. Viktor must have been the brains. The fact she'd escaped notice must just be luck.

The transaction lists didn't help me find her. Two cards showed a large cash advance on the day Viktor died, and after that, only the automatic withdrawals for the phone. It looked like she took the cash before someone might use the account to find her, but I couldn't rely on the exact timing. I'm sure someone would point out that maybe she put out the contract on her husband, but for someone with Viktor's background, I'm guessing ten grand was nowhere near enough to hire Viper.

I started digging into the phones. With the numbers and a bit of guessing at passwords — she used the numeric value of the two first names — I got access to the location services. Another hint that she wasn't a criminal mastermind, she should have turned off that feature.

Victoria Semenov and Cynthia Ilyich were both sitting in a diner in North Vancouver. If she was running, it was in the wrong direction. The interior was accessible from that side of the inlet, but it was a long way around and on a shitty road. Sure, the Vancouver Airport more than likely had high quality observation systems, but I would have headed up the Coquihalla, taken a plane from Kamloops or Kelowna to Alaska, then off the continent before the border closed to me.

I dropped my phone and the burner from Viper in my pocket and headed for my car. If Cynthia left the restaurant before I arrived, I could track her again. I wanted to talk to her before I called in the authorities. I might not be able to offer her a deal for talking, but I figured she would need some convincing before listening to Andy or David.

Cynthia sat in a booth in the corner farthest from the front door. The restaurant was dimly lit, so coming in from the sunshine meant I couldn't see anything for a few seconds. I guess my blindness benefited her. If she could get to the back door fast enough, no one would be able to ambush her. She didn't run when she saw me, so she must be looking for someone specific.

We'd only met the once when she played receptionist at the adoption agency office. She looked older now and resigned to a hard life, hair tied back in a ponytail, making her face look drawn, shoulders rounded. She stirred her drink with the tiny plastic sword. Maybe she wasn't running, just waiting for someone to kill her. The five little swords lined up on the table didn't bode well for her driving away.

I sat across from her, still no real reaction other than a slow blink.

"Are you running?" I had to know because I still hadn't figured out how to sell her on taking a deal.

"I haven't decided. Probably. Why?"

The decision would be out of her hands soon. "You remember me?"

"You are the bitch who ruined everything."

So not a fan. "I'm pretty sure Alan Blackhouse was about to screw everyone. But, fine. Yes, I put an end to the people trafficking. Your version of it, anyway."

"Our end was clean," Cynthia said. She lifted a pack of cigarettes from beside her and sniffed the contents. "I miss these. Why are you here?"

"I want to convince you to come with me to the cops. I think you have a better chance with them."

She pushed the pack away and took a sip of her drink. A pink half-frozen slop. Then she sat back against the booth. "It didn't work out so well for Viktor."

"No." I'd get nowhere arguing that point. "Ivan found him before we could set up the right protection."

"And you found me," she said. "How does that make me safe with the cops?"

Looking at the problem through my eyes wouldn't help. I might get pissed at the cops when I had to work around their rules, but fundamentally, I trusted them. As a criminal, maybe there was no one to trust. I tried to put my mind into her world view. "How does your plan keep you safe?"

She stirred her drink again, watching the trail of the sword point as it melted back into the slush. "How do you know I want to be safe?"

"You're hiding out here," I said. "If you didn't care, you'd kill yourself to make it easier, or find a way to make someone do it. You're thinking of running."

"Fair enough. You want me to tell-all for a deal that will in all likelihood backfire. How do you know I have something important enough?"

"Are you saying Viktor was in charge? You just did as he said?"

She licked her lips and smirked. "He was better at this than me, and he's dead. But I know some stuff. Enough for that Russian asshole to want me dead."

"Then you know enough to negotiate for a deal." I should have told Andy before I came so I'd know the parameters of a deal. All I had now was assurances, and Cynthia needed more than just promises to change her plans.

"I think I'll take my chances." She pushed her empty glass to the side and shoved the cigarettes into her purse.

"You can't drive after that many drinks."

"I have a ride and a plan." She looked at me and grunted. "You need to stop worrying about me. Or people like me. We walk into this life with our eyes open. I've been creating escape plans for years. I wasn't sure I'd actually get in the car when it arrived, but you convinced me it's my only real option."

She wanted to believe I'd talked her into it. Interesting. "Have you ever had to run before? Alone?"

"I'm not going to be alone," she said. "I don't need to trust anyone for long. I'll be working with a cartel, or another Russian before Kuznetsov's people find me. My new boss will protect me to ensure I keep his secrets."

"Aren't you afraid no one will take you on? I mean, losing the business hit Kuznetsov's revenue. Why would anyone else risk it?"

She checked her phone. "My ride is five minutes out. You need to be gone before then or he'll kill you."

We were done anyway, but I couldn't let it go. "You didn't answer my question."

"The Guptas and Blackhouse took the fall for that mess. I stay alive because I'm always behind the big players. I don't know what Viktor did to piss off Kuznetsov, but it had nothing to do with me."

"If I found you, he can." I couldn't reconcile this with the woman who left such an easy trail to follow.

"I don't care if he tracks me here. I'm gone, and I know how to be offline. You found me because I left a trail to here. To check if anyone was coming. No one came. Now I disappear."

She talked a big game, but I didn't see a weapon. She wasn't pretending to be drunk; I could smell the drink on her. If someone had come looking with intent to kill, she'd be dead. The fact that she could run from here had more to do with how high on Kuznetsov's list she sat than her knowledge or luck. "I don't know whether to hope I'm wrong and you'll live, or hope you are, and you'll die. Murder is wrong no matter what. But you living and continuing your business makes me sick."

"It doesn't matter. I live and keep doing my job, or I die and someone else does my job. As long as there's money to be made, someone will fill the void. Now go."

34

I sat in my car, waiting for Cynthia's ride to take her away. A silver SUV with tinted windows drove up, gave one honk and idled until she slipped through the door and into the back seat. She didn't even glance my way.

If I let her go, I'd be wondering if that was the right decision for a long time. I could follow the SUV. The road was pretty much a highway to the west. I could think of only a few places to the east for the driver to evade a tail. But what could I do? There was no place to hide, so the driver would see me if I tried for a picture of the license plate. Cynthia might already be dead, and the driver heading for a place to dump her body. I didn't need him, or her, coming back for me.

It was time to go back to David. I started the car and headed for the Lion's Gate Bridge.

THE BURNER PHONE rang as I exited the bridge. I grabbed it and answered. "Viper?"

"Who the fuck else?"

I risked getting pulled over by holding the phone while I drove. No intersections on the causeway, no kids playing on the sidewalk, so I was pretty safe.

"I tried to contact you."

"Yeah. I told you not to. Are you always stupid enough to annoy someone who can kill you when you aren't looking?"

"Then why did you put those contact numbers in?" I slowed for the traffic light at Georgia and Cardero.

"What did you want?"

"There's a contract on you." I stopped for the next red light. "I wanted to warn you. And to ask if you'll come in for a meeting with us. Get a deal."

Viper just laughed.

"Look, I know you think you can take care of yourself. I know other people who thought the same thing. If you can help the cops take down Kuznetsov, you can start over."

The call ended. I get that she didn't trust the cops — I barely did — but why give me a phone? Why would she want to talk to me if not to arrange a deal? And I could only think of two ways her future ran. Short and ended by a bullet to her head, or longer with a deal from some police force somewhere. The problem was her recent behavior had convinced me that I didn't know the criminal world enough to be sure who I could trust.

I WAS close to the RCMP offices when the burner rang again.

"What?" I didn't have the patience for her games.

"Arrange a meet. I will come to you. Send a text when you're ready."

"Wait. I can't guarantee what will happen, right? Don't play any tricks like at the park."

"When you contact me, you had better be able to guarantee safe passage. I'll handle the deal."

"And you have some information about Kuznetsov? That's what this is all about. We want him off the streets. We can look the other way over a lot of things, but if this is another game, you won't win." I drove into the parking lot and pulled over so I could talk.

"You want me to say I never killed anyone who didn't deserve it? I never killed kids or some other moral stance?"

It would be nice if she could, but even if all her targets were bad people, they still died by her hand. "If you said all that, I wouldn't believe you. Killing people for a living isn't okay, no matter what."

"An easy opinion when you got to choose a different life."

"Someone forced you to kill? Some secret spy organization trained you? You kill to protect your family? You couldn't do anything else well enough to survive?"

"No. You're right. I qualified as a doctor. But I had some bad habits. I found I was better at taking lives than saving them."

Was she trying to make a connection? I wasn't going to fall for it. Lies could sound like truth. Candor could be deceit. "When will you be ready to meet?"

"Within an hour."

"Fine. Anything else I should know before I call it in?"

"I have information that you can use. I won't spend time in prison. I'm very careful not to leave evidence."

The call ended.

Her words echoed in my head. If she'd told the truth, and maybe she did to get protection from whoever took the contract on her, then the case was almost over. But if she'd lied, the words could well be a threat. Not about past kills, but to warn us she would be very careful not to leave evidence when she killed us. If she found a way to slip a weapon past security, we'd be dead before anyone knew.

I had to trust the RCMP. They wouldn't give her a chance to do harm. We needed her information, and she had a reason to give it. And she could have killed me ten times over, but here I was, sitting in my car, getting ready to set up a meeting between the RCMP and a contract killer. Whoever said life is about making good choices didn't deal with criminals.

35

The coward in me wanted to call David and not go inside the building. I hated the coward because she never kept me from physical danger at the cost of my confidence. Her voice rang out every single time I faced a relationship conflict. She didn't want to fight with David face-to-face because you could always hang up on a call. I told her to shut up and pulled into an actual parking spot.

I sent a text that I was on my way and marched into the building.

In Andy's office, I explained the call from Viper.

"Where were you before that?" Andy asked. "I mean, she had to know you could take her call, so she was watching you."

I didn't want to tell them about Cynthia, but he had a point. I'd been so focused on making her safe that I wouldn't have noticed if a marching band of contract killers followed me. And maybe I needed to get past this knee-jerk mistrust of the good guys and trust of the bad guys.

"I met with Viktor's wife. I thought she might have something for us. Some way to take down Kuznetsov."

"Are you determined to get yourself killed?" Andy shouted.

I guess yelling meant he cared in some twisted way. David kept his eyes on the desktop, but I could see the color rising on his cheeks, and not from embarrassment. He was mad as hell but smart enough not to confront me here in public. That felt like love. With Andy it was more about control over me.

"I'm not even bruised. She told me no. She's gone into hiding — or she's dead in some ditch because she trusted the wrong person."

"And Viper?" David asked quietly. "Has she been watching you?"

"I don't know. Maybe she didn't care what I was doing when she called. But she's willing to talk if you agree not to arrest her as soon as you see her."

"No promises." Andy picked up a pen and started tapping it against the desk like a drumstick. "She definitely has something?"

"She says she does. Will she be safe to come here?"

Andy continued to drum the desk with the pen.

"Will Michel go for it?" David asked Andy before turning to me and saying, "It's not really up to Andy."

Michel Benoit would never agree to let a killer walk out of this building if she walked in. "Does he have to know?"

Andy dropped the pen in a drawer and sat straighter in his chair. "No, he'll want guarantees. We need to do it somewhere else. The VPD?"

David shrugged. "I can ask if we can borrow an interview room, but we'll have to sign her in. And I won't lie."

"Won't someone want to know why you need to borrow

a room?" I didn't believe the VPD would willingly give up the arrest of a known contract killer. They needed the good press.

"There isn't another place where we can interview and record with an observation room." Andy nodded to David. "You can at least ask, right?"

David turned away to make the call.

"So, the problem is just logistics," I asked. "You'll meet her and let her go?"

"We'll meet and see what she has to say," Andy said. "I'll agree not to arrest her if the information is worth it."

"No dice on the interview room," David said, turning back to us. "They've rounded up a bunch of gang members so they're working flat out."

I wanted to say we should rent an office. We can record on our phones. But Andy was thinking. If I interrupted him, he might say we'll agree and then arrest her as soon as she shows up.

"The images we took from the jail are not enough to identify her. We didn't get anything from the park meeting we can use in court. If Charity wants to press charges on the drug assault, it's the only charge to hold her on."

"Do you want me to?" It felt petty, but I didn't know where he was going with it.

David smiled. "No. He's saying we don't officially have anything to charge her with. Benoit might not like it, but without proof, we can't arrest her. Unless you want to."

"She'll get away with Viktor's death?" I blurted the question out without thinking. "I guess she's already done that if you can't prove anything."

"We'll keep the case open," Andy said. "Use it as leverage. We can make it difficult for her even if we can't press charges. Her work demands anonymity. If we decide to put the fuzzy image in the paper, no one will hire her. Or we can take a better image while she's with us."

"Are you saying we'll meet here?" I asked. "I need to confirm the details with her soon, or she'll be gone."

"Let me check Benoit's schedule." Andy opened a calendar on his laptop. I could see the screen reflected in the window.

"Benoit is in the building, but he's scheduled for a dinner meeting later. If we set it up so she comes in after he's gone, we'll avoid the trouble of convincing him."

Postpone it, more likely. I didn't care if Andy's boss ripped him a new one tomorrow. We were going to get a lead today. One that would take Kuznetsov off the streets.

"Tell her to come here, at nine. That gives us three hours to figure out what the hell we're going to ask her and what we can offer her in the way of reduced charges."

"I thought you couldn't charge her." I pulled out the burner phone.

"She doesn't know that," Andy said.

That's a big assumption.

"We don't know what she'll tell us," David added. "If she holds back because she's worried about incriminating herself, we won't get what we need."

I trusted they knew the best way to deal with her. I texted Viper the details. She responded, *I like my coffee sweet and black.*

36

We had time to eat something more than a quick sandwich, so Andy ordered takeout from a nearby Chinese restaurant. Gena and Luc joined us in the room, not exactly happy about closing the murder case, but happy to be on the team that was about to take down Ivan Kuznetsov. We all expected a fast result. Viper would give us evidence or point us in a direction. Then we'd bring Kuznetsov in for questioning, and he'd be off the streets. I wasn't the only one who thought it would go smoothly.

In the interview room, a coffee maker sat on the floor in a corner. Three comfortable chairs around a metal table with a bar across the center like some kind of hard-assed ping pong set up. The furniture reminded me what we were about to do, not talk with someone who could help us, but interrogate a suspect. Of course, Viper wouldn't be in handcuffs, so she wouldn't be attached to the bar. There was a slight odor of sour sweat, fear hormones I guess, and maybe that would make her feel more open to protection. At least we didn't have to eat in the room.

I finished my egg roll and wiped my greasy fingers on a napkin. "So, when we start, should I be her friend? I mean, she's probably not going to fall for the game but it's worth a try, right?"

"You won't be there." Andy tossed his paper plate in the recycle bin. "We'll meet her at the door and bring her to the room. We question her, and we get her to stick around until we're satisfied."

"I'm her contact." Why did he keep locking me out of things?

"And you did a great job, but you're done. Leave it to the professionals." Andy couldn't even look at me as he talked.

I turned to David, who shook his head. Gena and Luc found something in the chow mein container very interesting. I was on my own. "Why? What do you have that I don't?" I knew the easy answer — a badge or a gun or authority, but I wanted the truth. There was no reason I couldn't be part of the questioning.

"We know how to get information," David said. "You've helped get the case to this point. We got sidelined for a while by McCarthy's murder, but our goal was always Kuznetsov. And if you are there in the interview, a civilian, his legal team will use that to throw out the case."

Well, it was honest at least. I didn't want to be the reason Kuznetsov walked free, but it still felt like I'd been used. It was hard to miss out, but accepting the decision showed them that sometimes I could do the adult thing. "Can I watch?"

"No," Andy said. "Benoit is not going to like what we're doing. I don't need to add your presence to the load of shit he'll drop on me."

"Andy, she should observe." Gena was taking my side. "She might see something we don't. You know it's important to get more than one perspective. She'll be quiet. No one will know she's there."

"Do you think you can be invisible?" Andy asked me. "No questions. No knocking on the one-way glass, no sudden interruptions?"

If I said yes, of course, he wouldn't believe me. And he'd be right because I would interrupt if I thought they missed something. "What if I have something important?"

"Your boyfriend will be with you. This is going to be me and Gena. David and Luc will join you so you won't be alone."

It seemed fair. It was only Viper anyway — not that she was a model citizen or arresting her should be a priority. I wanted to be in the room when they took Kuznetsov down. If not with them, then observing would be enough. If I played well with the team now, maybe in the future they would cut me some slack.

"Okay. I can do that." I added a smile, but I don't think it reassured Andy. "What do we do now?"

He cleared the table and put his laptop on the desk. "Two hours until she shows. Assuming she doesn't play some kind of power game and comes early or late to put us off our stride. Take a break. If you can, take a nap. It's going to be a long night. Gena and I need to strategize."

I followed David and Luc out of the room. I wouldn't be able to sleep. Not because of the stress, or not completely because of it. I was a lousy napper.

"I have work to do on wrapping up the McCarthy case," Luc said. He waved and strode off.

"Walk?" David asked.

37

I t was a nice night, or as nice as a night can be in this part of town. The streets were busy, cars at the tail end of rush hour honking and crawling along. A few pedestrians, already drunk, and homeless people headed for the Oppenheimer Park tent city. David linked his arm in mine, and we headed back towards Crab Park.

"You did good work," he said, giving me a squeeze.

"I don't feel like it," I said.

"You don't like to play within the rules. Probably why you're so good at your job, but now Andy can't risk you acting on a hunch."

I sighed. I knew it was true, but I couldn't help feeling used. "I think my days of working on a team are coming to an end."

He gave me another squeeze. "I'll be happy when you're back to chasing insurance cheats."

I would be too. The adrenalin rush from catching the big bad guys wasn't worth the hassle.

We headed back to the office when we arrived at the edge of the park. This was not a good place at night. Having a break, even a short one, from the constant worry I'd be shoved out of the investigation let me relax enough to shut everything off until the interview.

David left me at the door to the observation room. "I'll check in with my sergeant."

He'd be back on the regular cop work soon, too. I slipped in and bagged the best chair, dropped my bag in the corner, and took out my phone to play games for a while.

A call came through. Unknown number. Viper calling the meeting off?

"Ivan is watching you." A man's voice.

"Who is this?"

"Someone close to him. He doesn't want to kill you. Too much trouble. But he will. You need to stop."

"Why are you warning me?"

"He is getting out of control. He's bringing attention from the bosses. I don't want to die because I didn't stop him. I don't want to die trying to stop him either."

"So, warning me is your way of saving your ass?"

"You might slow him down until we can get out of the crossfire. You be careful."

38

Kuznetsov getting closer to me should be scary, but I was in the RCMP office in an observation room. He couldn't kill me here. And other people could do a lot more damage to his plans than me. And killing me would bring on a ton of retribution. So, I didn't tell anyone about the call. I mean, if the henchman reported to Kuznetsov's boss, maybe we'd find Ivan's body before we found him alive. I'm pretty sure I was trying to convince myself with logic to quiet the skitter of fear over my skin.

Now I sat with David watching Viper get settled across the table from Andy and Gena. Viper sipped the coffee and nodded. "Good."

"You have information to help us take down Kuznetsov?" Gena asked.

"I do. What's the offer? I'm not handing over information for free." Viper checked her cuticles like she didn't care.

"We can't let you go." Andy pushed a sheet of paper toward Viper. "We'll give you a new identity. Your sentence will be minimal, but you will do time."

"Then I should leave now. Tell Charity it was nice to meet her." She didn't move.

"You want to walk away from here after killing who knows how many people?" Gena asked.

I thought we had all this worked out before she got here. "What are they doing?"

"She needs to play this game to believe we're serious," David said. "If we told her she could get away with killing McCarthy by giving us Kuznetsov, she wouldn't believe it."

"So, she needs to bargain?" It made a weird kind of sense. They let Viper believe she'd negotiated a better deal, and she lets something slip.

"It builds a weird kind of trust." David pointed to the paper on the table. "That's the minimum the Crown thought we'd get away with. There's a better offer ready, but as usual, we are under orders to give up the least we can for the most information. Whatever we end up with, Viper gets a new identity and a pass on a bunch of charges we can't prove. We get Kuznetsov."

"You think she might know who his replacement is?" Until now, when we came so close to capturing him, I hadn't thought much about the future. The crime wouldn't go away, too lucrative. Were we changing out a demon for the devil?

"Interpol or someone will know for sure. But we might get lucky," David said. "Some of the new guys are more into business than random violence. They make deals and only kill as a last resort."

"That's not better," I said. "Just quieter."

"We take what we can get. She's getting ready to deal."

While we'd talked, Viper and Gena bonded — I guess. Andy took a back seat and let Gena run the interview.

"I will tell you what I know, and you let me walk away. I

don't need your protection. It won't help. I need Kuznetsov busy while I disappear. I won't go to your court. I won't give a statement."

Gena leaned forward on the desk, not threatening but including Viper in a secret. "We need the information. You stay in here until we get Kuznetsov off the streets."

Viper shrugged. "I am hungry."

For someone who wanted to help, the woman was being a complete asshole. I don't know if it was her request for food, or the whole 'I'm doing you a favor' attitude, but I wanted someone to lock her up until she came to her senses.

"Do you agree to the offer?" Andy said. He took out his phone. "I can order something in."

"Pizza. Good pizza with pepperoni. And beer," she said. "I agree to stay with you until you get your proof, or for two days. If you can't use my information before that, I will leave. You will not follow me."

Andy ordered food. "The guards will make sure it's safe."

"Why don't you want to take our protection?" Gena asked.

Viper barked a quick laugh. "I can take care of myself."

Andy put his phone on the table. "Okay. Time to show us what you have."

"You think I wrote it down? Or I took incriminating pictures? I don't keep records. No professional does. If I need to prove the job is done, I use a burner to send a picture, then I drop the burner off a bridge or something."

"So you tell us," Gena said. "You give us whatever you think is valuable enough to us and we see what happens."

"First I need to eat and sleep." Viper sat back and crossed her arms. "Tomorrow."

"Why is she stalling?" I asked.

"She must have a reason, because she came in. It might be to mess with us, but it doesn't feel like that's the reason." David frowned. "Maybe she's tired. If she knows she can leave when she wants to, it's a good place to sleep and recharge."

Gena turned to Andy. "Maybe we should arrest her for McCarthy's murder. We have more cooperative witnesses."

I wouldn't call Dean a cooperative witness.

"We can give her time," Andy said. "Send the pizza to the break room. She can nap there. We'll start again in two hours."

"Tomorrow." Viper stood. "This break room sounds like a good idea."

Andy didn't contradict her on the timing. He opened the door. Three officers escorted Viper away.

I stepped out of the observation room, David right behind me. "I think she's just leading us on."

"You might be right," Gena said. "Maybe she's keeping us focused here while something happens outside. Something that will let her get away clean."

"No, not to keep us distracted," Andy said. "To pull power games, probably. But maybe to give herself an alibi for something that's going to happen."

I didn't like the sound of that. "You mean so she can't be accused of another assassination?"

"Maybe." Gena rubbed her eyes. "I need a nap too. I should be able to figure this out, but my brain is out of ideas."

"Remember, Kuznetsov put a hit on her," David said. "She has every reason to hide out with us for a couple of days."

"So, she's dragging it out, hoping he'll forget about the contract?"

"Yes," David said. "She doesn't want our help. She can't string us along with bad information, or not for long. She'll tell us what she has soon enough, and then she'll be gone."

I hoped he was right.

39

We were back in Andy's office with coffee. It was late, but we weren't going to sleep anyway. I couldn't stop turning the interview over in my head. Why did Viper come in only to stall?

"Maybe she's not here to establish an alibi," I said. "What if she's here to ride out whatever's happening on the streets?"

"Not the hit," David said. "Unless she expects it to be canceled soon."

I didn't think she wanted to hide here to avoid a contract killer. I mean, it wouldn't happen here, but she was planning to leave. So, the killer only needed to be patient. "Why would Kuznetsov cancel a hit?"

"Sometimes, the contract is just a threat," Andy said. "Kuznetsov might be telling her that she's not protected. Sometimes things change and the kill isn't good for business. Sometimes the person who put out the contract dies."

She thinks one of those things is about to happen. It feels right. "Does the assassin sometimes kill the client?"

"I don't think we hear about it officially. But if a client tried to renege on the payment, it could happen."

Hiding seemed like a very passive way for Viper to survive.

Andy's desk phone rang.

The caller couldn't have said more than two sentences. Andy hit the speaker and said, "Put him on."

David and I perked up.

"Blackhouse violated his agreement. Went out to a club because he was bored," Andy said as we waited.

Alan Blackhouse was crazy. Or he'd gone crazy in the days before his arrest. His deal was sweet, and he decided to go to a club?

"I'm done," Alan said by way of introduction.

"It doesn't work that way," Andy said. "You don't cooperate, you go to trial. You go to prison for a long time."

"You going to give me the speech about what they do to people like me in prison? Selling kids?"

Andy looked up at the ceiling and closed his eyes for a breath. "I don't care what your fellow prisoners will do. Not my job to keep you safe unless you stick to the rules."

"You can't make me safe. Kuznetsov is out of control. He's going to take down a lot of people when he goes. I won't be going to jail. I'll be in the morgue, or I'll find a way to disappear."

Is that what he was doing in the club? Making arrangements? I kept my question to myself. Andy was trying to get Alan back in the fold.

"Are you sure you want to back out of the deal?" Andy asked. "If Kuznetsov is cleaning house, you might want to stay put for a while."

"I said you can't protect me," Alan shouted. "I'm done."

"Fine. Take him in." Andy waited for confirmation, then we all listened to Alan arguing about being cuffed. Andy hung up on the idiot.

"Charity, you aren't safe now," Andy said. "Alan's deal meant you didn't need to testify to the child trafficking case."

"Great. Now I'm a real target." I was before, but not at the top of what I hoped was a long list. Now? I'm guessing I got promoted to top ten. "If he's right, Viper is here to ride out the mess Kuznetsov is about to make."

"We might be wrong," David said. "She might be here to kill you to make up for her mistakes."

"She would have killed me in the park." That wasn't the only time she could have taken my life.

"You will go into protection," Andy said. "You are not a consultant now; you are a material witness."

"No. Somehow Alan knew what was going on. They got to him. He's right about protection. If Kuznetsov wants to get at me, he will."

"If a contract killer comes in to hide, what makes you think you can take care of yourself?" David touched my hand as if that would soften what I heard him say.

"Look. We need to get him off the streets, and I'm part of that. I'll wear a vest, be with an escort all the time, whatever you want bar hiding in here." *Please don't call my bluff.*

"Have you been threatened?" David asked.

"Not by Kuznetsov," I said. Then realizing I was skating past the line, I added, "Warned. But all vague."

"We need to talk to Viper again," Andy said. "Until we do, you are staying here."

So, I was safe enough for now as long as I stayed inside the building. Until I tried to leave, we avoided the fight.

Viper was sleeping when we walked into the break

room. Andy woke her so we could escort her to the interview room. This time, David and I stayed.

"You don't have anything on Kuznetsov," Andy said.
"You're hiding here until the shit is over."

"So, you think you know everything," Viper said. "Yes.
Staying here is safer for me. I left it too late to escape the
country, so I found a haven."

"And you have no information for us?" I asked. If Andy
didn't want to update her on Alan, I was happy to keep
quiet.

"I know something, but you must decide what it's
worth."

"Time to hand it over," Andy said. "You were right that
we probably don't have enough to charge you, but this is not
a hotel."

He'd throw her out into the street when there was a
contract on her life?

"Yes, he's cleaning house, but he'll do it in order. First,
anyone who worked for him and might be a danger. Then
some rivals. Then he'll try to take more business from the
locals. After that, he'll be done."

"And Charity?" David asked. "Where does she fit into the
plan?"

Viper looked at me and pursed her lips in thought.
"Behind me, I think. He knows killing a cop's girlfriend is
going to bring a pile of retribution and attention. He's not
that far out of control." It was hard to ignore the unspoken
yet.

I smiled at David and Andy. Viper had just made my
argument for me. I was safe until a lot of bad people died.
That would take Kuznetsov a while.

"How will he try to take more of the business?" Andy
asked.

"Two ways to do it. He makes a deal for a very big slice of their profits, and he lets them live. Or he pretends to make a deal, gets the leaders together and kills them."

40

Being up all night got harder as I got older. I needed real coffee and some kind of pastry. Since Viper confirmed I wasn't in immediate danger, I wanted to get out of the building. Not permanently, but it wouldn't be long before Andy stuck me in protective custody, so this might be my last chance.

I checked on my phone for all-night coffee places and found one a few blocks away. "Time for a coffee run."

Andy looked at me like I was insane. David sighed and shook his head slowly like a man defeated before he started.

"I'm safe. Just two blocks there and back. The streets are empty at this time of the morning."

"No." Andy seemed to think I would suddenly become obedient.

"Am I under arrest?" I knew he was right about it being dangerous, but I needed to be out of the office and alone so I could think.

"You don't need to make him lock you up, Charity," David said. "I want you on the phone with me at all times."

"I said no," Andy insisted.

David waved away Andy's objections. "She's going to do it, and arguing won't stop her."

"What do you want me to bring back?" I asked. For a change, I didn't fight a battle I'd already won. "I promise to do what David asked. I won't take unnecessary risks."

"This whole thing is an unnecessary risk." Andy looked at Viper. "If she gets hurt, I'm holding you responsible."

"Why? I think she's stupid to go out." Viper grinned at me. If she meant for me to be reassured, she missed the mark.

"I'm taking orders now," I said.

FIVE MINUTES later I walked along the street. I loved the early hours in the city. It was actually quiet. Only three cars in sight on a usually heavily trafficked road. The air smelled cleaner, even though I knew it couldn't be. The stab- and bullet-proof vest I wore hugged me tight. I'd charged my earphones, and my phone rested in my pocket. All was well with the world.

"Talk to me," David said.

"I feel like an idiot talking to myself."

"No one can see you," he said. "And I'm not going to wait until something goes wrong to hear your voice."

"Sweet. The coffee shop is right ahead. The sign is lit. I'll be inside in a few seconds."

"Anyone else out there?"

It hadn't occurred to me that someone could be hiding. But now I felt the skin on my back crawling. I stopped and leaned against a shop door to pretend to adjust my shoe. "I don't see anyone."

"Just wait a second," David said. "We'll send a patrol car around the block."

Suddenly the quiet street felt menacing. The darkness was deeper between the streetlights. The coffee shop was across the road, and a car could come around the intersection, men in masks and dark clothing could jump out and grab me.

The patrol car cruised past, and the officer inside gave me the thumbs up.

"They say the street's clear," David confirmed.

A shadow moved in a doorway across the street. "They might be wrong."

"If you think so, come back," David said.

I slowed my breathing, trying to avoid the panic building in my gut. If I was being followed, it didn't need to be connected to Kuznetsov. Muggers and perverts existed outside the current crisis and always would.

The coffee shop lights were bright. Music drifted out of the doorway. My nerves settled and the crawling feeling faded. I could do this. If this was a hit, they wouldn't be tailing me. The walk to this point had provided plenty of opportunities for a bullet.

I gave myself a pep talk. I'm wearing protection. If we can catch whoever is following me, it might give us a step forward in the case. I was not a wuss. I put myself here, and if I turned around and ran back to the RCMP, I would never forgive myself. And they would never let me out again.

"Charity, say something." David's voice interrupted my process.

"I'm okay." He wasn't going to like my next words, but I had try to get a look at whoever trailed me. "I think someone is there. Don't send that patrol car again."

"Come back."

"No. We need to be sure."

Silence. I waited for a siren and two burly cops to drag me to safety.

"What's your plan?"

"I don't know."

"Is anyone else on the street?"

I looked around to make sure, but I was alone — or, not completely if someone was lurking. "I can hear something going on a bit ahead."

"Can you wait somewhere safe?"

"The coffee shop is the only thing open. It won't work if I hide in there, too well-lit and it's small."

"Give me a minute to figure something out. Stay on the line and tell me if anyone comes near."

I agreed and pulled my phone out of my pocket to make it obvious I was talking to someone. Maybe discourage whatever my shadow planned. The noises from beyond the coffee shop were still constant, but I couldn't think why anyone would be gathered out here this late. The homeless people had tents up in a few parks, but there was nothing in that direction but retail and offices.

David's voice came through the phone, but he wasn't talking to me. Andy said something, then Gena, then David. They were coming up with a plan.

The shadow I'd noticed didn't reappear. Why would it? I was stationary, no need to follow if I didn't move. I shouldn't stare at the location and give away my interest. I scanned the area, pretending to look for an address on my phone.

The vest was starting to feel like a vise, and my ears started ringing.

"Charity, we have a plan. Are you still up for it?"

"Yes. Anything other than standing here like a target."

41

The plan was simple. I go for a little walk toward the noise. They put a tail on me to find whoever followed me, if anyone did. When we know, I buy the coffee and return. Part of me wanted to be ordered back to safety, but only a small part, and if I gave into the fear, my career as a PI would be over.

I straightened up, took a deep breath, regretted it as I tasted the air, and started strolling toward whatever was happening ahead. I controlled the urge to look around for either my stalker or my protection. If they were good, I wouldn't see anyone.

The patrol car passed again as I reached the corner. Neither of the occupants looked my way. They could just be on their usual beat, nothing to do with me, but I felt the last hooks of tension release in my shoulders knowing that help was nearby.

The noise came from a party that spilled out of a storefront and onto the sidewalks. Big white trucks parked across the street, and banks of lights shone down. Not a party — Hollywood North. Usually, a security team guarded the shoots, but tonight they needed crowds and at this time, pedestrians were few and far between. A young woman in a tee shirt with a production logo splashed across the front walked toward me.

"Hi. Would you like to be in the show?" She held out a clipboard with a release form attached. "We'll keep you in the background, so no need to fix your hair or make up."

This crowd would be the best cover for me. A lot of witnesses to keep a killer at bay. I still had to walk back to the station, but I'd know either way whether it was safe because being here gave David time to clear any dangers. I signed the form and followed her directions to mill about on the edge of the party.

Some of the people I joined were experienced extras. A man drew me close and whispered instructions while we waited for the director to start the scene.

"You follow our lead," he said. "Don't cross in front of the talent. Do exactly what you're told and nothing more."

I knew this from watching my ex-boyfriend, but I wanted him to think me a total newbie. "Thanks. This is kind of fun."

"It's work, honey. You know you get paid, right? No one works for free, or the bastards will stop paying anyone."

"Got it. How much?" I asked the question because I thought a person wandering into a shoot would ask.

"Three fifty minimum." He looked me up and down. "Can you take your jacket off? If you can look different, they can use you more."

"Look different?"

He puffed out a breath like he couldn't believe how stupid I was. "If you wander around in the same clothes for different scenes it ruins the magic."

If I wandered around in a stab- and bullet-proof vest it

would do the same. "No. I guess they won't need me for long."

He grabbed my shoulder and turned me to face the actors. "Pay attention, we're about to be on."

The director called for quiet, and someone yelled, "Rolling."

My buddy nudged me to follow him as he joined two other extras and pretended to hold a conversation. One of them started vaping and another lit up what looked and smelled like a real joint. Two minutes later, we stood down while they adjusted something for the next take.

"What is this show?" I'd seen filming before when I dated Jake. He's an actor, and his career took off shortly before he dumped me — in the nicest way. There was never a sign to say the title of the movie or TV show shooting, only a working title acronym on directions to parking for crew.

"Some crime thing," my buddy said. "Set in Toronto. I think the guy over there in the tee shirt and leather pants is supposed to be a Russian gangster trying to turn a leaf."

How would they know if a real Russian mobster came on set? "Who's the production company?"

My buddy frowned at me before he decided to answer. "You sure know a lot for a newbie. Some European group is fronting the money. The guy who comes on set yelling about costs is their lawyer. Popov."

I should have left my phone recording and not turned it off like the girl told me after I signed the waiver. Popov was the lawyer we suspected of ties to Kuznetsov. I wasn't egotistical enough to think this whole setup was about me, but being here was too dangerous. If Popov knew me and showed up to check on my movements, I had nowhere to hide.

I grabbed for my phone.

"Hey, you can't use that on set," the vaping extra said.

"I guess I have to leave the set, then."

I saw the clipboard girl hurrying over. She must have Spidey senses about phones. I stepped away from the lights and she followed.

"Give me that phone." She held out her hand.

"No. I need to make a call."

"You signed a waiver. No phones on set."

"I'm off the set now," I said, pointing to the barriers we'd just passed.

She glared at me.

"Look, rip up the paperwork. I'm not who you need for background work."

She lifted my waiver off the clipboard. "I'll make sure no one hires you for extra work again."

Like that was going to stop me making a call. But it was a good threat to make with professionals who needed the work. A professional wouldn't be in this position. My thoughts were babbling, and I needed to get away, so I glared back. "Rip it up or not. I'm leaving."

A black SUV pulled up across the street. A bald man dressed in white pants, white shirt and white shoes stepped out. I recognized the face. Popov. I slipped farther away from the lights. I remembered that no one had interviewed him, but he definitely looked like a mob lawyer. It seemed pretty convenient that he showed up at a shoot this early in the morning just when I arrived.

I called David to let him know about Popov showing up and he told me to wait for an escort. "Don't let him see you. Luc will be there to bring you back here."

42

I'm not sure what I expected when we walked into the break room, but it definitely wasn't Andy ordering a handful of officers around. The place should be calm. We had Viper ready to cooperate. The case would be over in a few hours if we were lucky.

David pulled me into a hug as soon as he saw me, but I only let it go on for a few seconds. I shouldn't need comfort. His arms around me felt so good though.

"What's happened?" I asked the room in general.

"That stupid guard is dead," Viper said. "Someone was not watching closely, or maybe another dishonest employee. I can't say for certain, and your friends are pissed off."

I plunked the coffee tray on the table and sat. I hadn't really thought Dean was in danger. He didn't know much, if anything. Kuznetsov's priorities must be different from what we assumed. I wondered about Cynthia again. I hoped she was right, and her plan worked despite what she did before. I'd had my fill of death. Nothing I could do for her anyway.

"How?" I asked David. "Do we know who did it? Is anyone else hurt?"

He sat beside me and took my hand. "Just him. We're still trying to figure out how the killer got near him. I hope Viper is wrong, but if someone didn't take a payment to look the other way, it means the protection detail was incompetent. That's worse."

There had to be another explanation. "Did they shoot him?" Maybe a sniper. Anything would be better than incompetence.

"No, stabbed. Very much like Viper's technique." David glared at her as he spoke.

"Good thing she's in custody." I was at sea here. Yes, I'd been warned that Kuznetsov was out of control. Yes, I expected him to target people in his effort to shut down the investigation. But was Dean low-hanging fruit or were our assumptions wrong? If we couldn't figure out Kuznetsov's plans, more people would die before we shut him down.

"We'll have a video of the scene in two minutes," Andy said.

The rest of the cops were gone. Off on some search for clues, I figured. "Why don't we go down there?"

"I want Viper to see it, and she's not getting outside our doors until we've got Kuznetsov."

He sounded like he believed that he exerted some control over her. I guessed we had her until she decided to leave. If she had an insight into this murder, I didn't care who was right.

"I will try to help," Viper said. "It is in my best interest, after all. I imagine the killer was looking for me."

"Why would Kuznetsov target Dean right now?" I asked.

"You assume there are no other bodies waiting to be found?" Viper gave me a cold smile.

So he could be far down his list of people to kill. "It's going to be expensive to take out all the threats." The money would not be a problem. He didn't even have to launder the funds to pay for a hit.

"He has his own men," Andy said.

My imagination filled with images of an army of gangsters killing their way through the city. Like some demented comic book.

"Here's the video," Gena said. She moved aside as we crowded around her laptop.

The room was basic; a bed, an easy chair with a side table, and a dresser with a TV on top. A cheap motel. "I thought you put him in a secure location."

"We wanted him kept secret." Andy pointed to the screen. "Body is at the morgue already. Blood on the covers. The security detail stationed outside the room said no one went in. Only one entrance."

"Is there security footage?" David asked. "Someone went into the room unless they screwed up clearing it."

"The cameras went off-line for a half hour," Gena said. "Every thirty minutes the guards go in and check on Dean. Up to the last time, then we have no footage until they went in for the regular check and found him dead."

Viper shoved me out of the way to get closer to the screen. "He used my method — hypothetically — and he drugged your guards. Plenty of chemicals that would put them out for long enough to do this. Or perhaps, just wipe their memories."

"You know who killed him?" I didn't buy the idea that two RCMP constables got drugged and didn't notice. Yes, they could be taken out, but when they woke up, how did they miss the fact that they were lying on the floor?

"There is one man I've heard about. His method is to mimic others. I suppose he thinks that it will confuse an investigation if he gets caught. Let him point to other kills he couldn't have done."

"Do you use drugs to gain access?" I asked. I mean she used drugs to confuse me in the park, but I wanted to hear what she'd say.

"Don't try to trick me into a confession."

I rolled my eyes. "If you hypothetically needed to commit murder, would you hypothetically use drugs?"

She didn't look away from the scene. "Yes. There are drugs like rohypnol that can be used in a spray. They are short lived, hard to find in a drug screen, and don't incapacitate. The right dose would remove a section of memory. And maybe make them easy to manipulate."

"Get security footage from the neighboring businesses if there is any," Andy said. "We should be able to find something."

Gena turned off the video and left us to follow Andy's orders.

"Name?" David asked.

"Of the assassin?" Viper reached into the bag of donuts I'd brought with the coffee. "He's known as The Wraith. I have no idea who he really is. We don't have meetings or hang out together in a bar after work for a bitch session."

"What else do you know about him?" I asked. Even if all she had were rumors, we needed data to make any progress.

"He's weird. He will take on jobs just for the thrill. And he's old. Maybe this is his way of retiring? Taking on a big package of contracts. Get paid big. Disappear."

"Or he could be the one out of control," I said.

"If that is the case, you're all going to be killed."

43

"There's not much we can do today," Andy said.

We'd left Viper in the break room with a guard and regrouped in Andy's office.

"Maybe a good idea to go home and sleep. For a couple of hours," David said. "Who's investigating Dean's murder?"

Andy closed down his computer and started locking away the various hard copies on his desk. "Gena and Luc. The VPD has enough on its hands. They didn't put up much of a fight."

Having our people take the case made sense to me. I'd be surprised if the killing turned out to be unrelated. They also had access to Viper in case they had questions. I couldn't imagine Andy actually following through and giving anyone outside the team access to her. She'd find a way to slip out when any strangers left. Not that we could hold her if she insisted on walking out, but we weren't done with her yet.

I turned to David. "Are you coming home?"

He nodded, and I saw exhaustion weighing him down.

"Three hours at home puts us back here at nine?" I picked up my phone to set an alarm. Three hours wouldn't be enough, but it was more sleep than we'd had in a couple of days. Power naps kept me going, but not at my peak. My own bed rather than a couch sounded like heaven.

"I'll be back in a minute," David said.

"I need to prep Gena and Luc," Andy said. "Let's make it ten o'clock, here in my office. We're getting Viper's information and putting an end to Kuznetsov before the end of the day."

He sounded positive, like he could bring the case to an end through sheer will.

I started packing my bag as soon as he left me alone. I hoped to get a moment with Viper before I left, but I didn't want David or Andy to catch me. She was holding back something vital. I wanted her to tell me why. I mean, I wanted to know what, but hoped she'd explain why, and the answer would put us on a path to getting Kuznetsov off the streets.

My phone rang as I dropped it into my bag. I dug it out from the bottom before the call went to voicemail. "Yes?" I forgot to look at the ID. A sign of how tired I was.

"You forgot your jacket." A male voice. I didn't recognize it, but there were a lot of people in this case I didn't know. Including the new contract killer and Kuznetsov. But someone was watching me here. And the window didn't offer a great angle for someone to spy from the outside.

He'd waited until I was alone, so I couldn't alert anyone. "I didn't grab it yet. Where are you?"

"Not far. You got away from me on the street. But when I'm ready, you'll meet me."

I knew someone could triangulate the caller's location if

I held him on the call long enough. "So, I'll see your face? Not a bullet?"

"No. My employer told me to make you personal."

"Kuznetsov? He gave you instructions?"

"Good guess, but then, how many people might want you dead?"

"You'd be surprised. Why are you calling?"

"So you know I'm watching you. I like my victims to stew a bit."

The call ended. I ran to the break room. Andy was there with Viper.

"Where's David?"

"Here," he said, stepping into the room behind me. "We just heard that Blackhouse is dead."

"How? I thought he was being watched."

"This time they clearly drugged a guard," David said. "Whoever did it cleared the security footage too. We can't trust our usual methods to keep people safe."

"He decided to violate his deal," I said. "I should feel bad about his death, but I don't. He had every chance to help, and he only thought about himself."

"I'm not sure the official story will take that into account. At least we're safe here."

I told them about the call. "I think the office might be bugged."

Andy started swearing as he tapped a message into his phone. When he finished texting and swearing, he looked up and said, "I'll have the office swept, but it could have been a drone from outside."

I hadn't even thought of a drone. "He said he was following me before."

"Yes," David put his arm around me. "And now we get to

stay here. I want you safe. We can rest here as easily as at home."

My normal knee-jerk reaction to being protected was absent. Maybe because I really needed sleep, or maybe because I'm not that stupid. "I agree. Not forever."

"You want my opinion?" Viper sat watching us with a smirk. "You will be killed last. This one, he wants to play around with you like a cat with a spider."

"I'm not taking chances," Andy said. "Tomorrow, we need you to tell us everything."

"Sure," Viper said. "Unless something comes up. I think tomorrow will be a good day for us to work."

Andy was right. We were too worn out to make sense of anything. The shock of the call left me empty. "Where am I sleeping?"

"Benoit's office. It has two couches." He reached for my phone. "I need that so the techs can to try to locate your caller."

I didn't want to hand over my only way of researching. My laptop was in my bag, but no way would I be able to sit up and work. He curled his fingers in, beckoning the phone to his palm. I sighed and gave it to him. "I need that back."

"Before we start again," Andy said. "You don't need the distraction now; you need sleep."

"You think Viper is right?" I asked David as a uniformed officer escorted us to Benoit's office. "That I'm safe for a while?"

He put his arm around my shoulders and gave me a gentle squeeze. "I can't be sure. But think of it this way; nothing significant changed. You are still on a list of people Kuznetsov wants dead. He got a look at you in the nightclub before we raided. And you are on-line, so he wouldn't have to work hard to get an image to pass on to a contract killer."

Maybe all that was true, but something had changed. I was scared now. I hoped desperately that a few hours' sleep would wash the fear away. I planned on being an active part of the takedown, even if I had to bully myself to make it happen.

44

W hen we regrouped later that morning, my fear had changed into anger and determination to take Ivan Kuznetsov off the streets. I didn't care that someone else would step in to fill his role; that person wouldn't be looking to kill me personally. The sweep of Andy's office came up clean, so the asshole who called must have been using a drone.

We had breakfast sandwiches and coffee laid out on the break room table. And Viper had just joined us. She'd spent the night in a guarded but unlocked holding cell, so we'd know she couldn't slip away, yet she wouldn't feel trapped.

"Time to give us your information," Andy said. "We need Kuznetsov locked down."

"Okay," Viper said, wiping ketchup from her cheek. "Your main problem is you don't know where he is, right?"

If she had even a hint of an idea where Kuznetsov was hiding out, she should have told us before more people got killed. I kept my thoughts inside. Was she lying? Was it some kind of delaying tactic?

"Yes. We raided the nightclub he used for a base, and he cleared out. No sightings of him since then."

Viper tilted her head as though an idea surprised her. "Are you sure you are still dealing with him and not a new player?"

I didn't believe her for a second. If Kuznetsov had been taken out by his gang, they would want to send a message to everyone that he'd crossed a line.

"You think this is a new boss?" David asked. "Cleaning house?"

Viper looked in her empty mug, then at the coffee maker.

I got up and started a cup brewing. If she was going to play games, I'd let her for a while. Her information would be useful; I had to believe it. If she was stringing us along, we were lost. Maybe Andy or David had a plan. I couldn't concentrate on one plan because I needed so many to solve my problems. I was being watched; I was on a hit list. I would be locked in here for the rest of my life.

I pushed the full mug toward her. "Start talking." Maybe this was her game. Playing with the real cops. She might respond to me since I didn't carry a badge — and she seemed to like me.

"I know Kuznetsov's location. When we set up the kill, he didn't take enough precautions," she said. "I took the call. I recognized the sound of float planes landing. Only one place that happens."

"Richmond." Andy texted someone. "Is that all? Or can you pinpoint it closer?"

Only a few places in Richmond do you hear those kinds of planes landing. "Terra Nova. Still a big area."

"I have more. What will you give me in trade?"

Before she could answer, Gena joined us, pointing a remote at the TV in the corner. "You need to see this."

The local twenty-four-hour news came on. The scrolling text across the bottom read, *four dead in suspected gang violence.*

"Who's on the case?" David asked. "We need to see the scenes."

"Only one scene," Gena said. "A house in Richmond. We'll take the case over, but at the moment your pals at VPD are on it."

If the killer was Kuznetsov, or someone he hired, had he burned his newest hideout? "Can we ask for pictures?" I asked. "There must be something at the scene to help us."

David sent a text and got a response right away. "Got them. Not all, but the overview of the three spots. Two killed in a bedroom. One on the stairs, and one in the kitchen."

"Send them to me," Gena said. "We can look at them on my laptop. Back in a sec."

I looked at the screen again. "Any idea where he's going next?" I asked Viper. "That house was probably where he called from."

"I must look at the images," she said. "It will help me guess to see what was left behind."

Gena rejoined us. "They've got IDs on two of the victims. Local gang leaders, Fallen Lotus."

She opened the images, and we crowded around. The first was the body on the stairs. Blood everywhere. Like someone had bludgeoned him to death. His head a bloody pulp, they'd need DNA to identify him. The second image was the bedroom. The two bodies laid out on the rug, face up. Young men, maybe mid-twenties, throats cut, and chests stabbed multiple times. "The gang members?"

"Yeah. I think we're supposed to recognize them," Gena said.

The final body in the kitchen was pinned to the floor with what looked like iron fence posts. Face up, blond with a Van Dyke goatee. "I've seen him before. One of Kuznetsov's men," I said. He was of the henchmen in the nightclub.

"No one sanctioned this," Viper whispered. "I've done work for Russians. A lot of work. But they don't do this to their own."

"The man on the stairs, can they tell if he's Asian?"

David sent another text. He looked at the answer. "No. Pale skinned. Russian gang tattoos all over his upper body."

"Get Luc and go take over the scene right away," Andy told Gena. "We need full control of this."

I needed to practice their trick of catnapping. Gena didn't even look tired after all this time.

"Why would Kuznetsov do this?" I asked Viper. "If you're right, and it's not the kind of thing his bosses would condone? It makes no sense."

"I don't know. This is not a contract kill." She leaned in and brought up the image from the kitchen again. "He might suspect betrayal? Do you have someone undercover?"

"If we did, we wouldn't need you," Andy said. "If Kuznetsov is going on a killing spree, there's a reason."

"I did get a call from one of his people," I said. I waited to be yelled at for keeping secrets again, but no one spoke. Maybe I'd worn them down. "Warning me. I think he was really working for the bosses, not Kuznetsov."

He'd been undercover, but reporting to the people running the whole gang, not the cops. People who controlled criminal activities worldwide. Was it normal for someone to be planted into a local operation? Spying on their own felt like a very Russian thing to do. But if it wasn't normal, why do it for Kuznetsov? And what would the rest of his henchmen think of the murder? If they deserted him, maybe this case would be over soon because he had no protection. If Kuznetsov still holds sway in the gang, this was just the start.

45

I couldn't decide whether I wanted to go to the murder scene or go looking for Ivan. Knowing they wouldn't let me in the house didn't make any difference. If I could see the details in person, maybe I'd find a clue no one else would be able to recognize.

"If he's cleaning house, how long before he gets me?" Viper sounded like she was talking to herself. Thinking through her options.

"You and Charity are safe here," Andy said. "He's not going to march in, shooting anyone who gets in his way. His pet assassin can't sneak in either."

I never realized before how hard it is to think when you are terrified and angry. I'm not stupid. I know how risky it was for me to go outside this building. But I didn't agree with Andy. We were no safer here than anywhere. Twice Kuznetsov got someone into a secure environment to commit murder.

Viper was still weighing the risks. She knew the same thing I did. And she had resources outside the building to help her. My options were limited to in here, or in VPD protective custody. At least here, I might be able to convince someone I could help with the case.

Andy closed the laptop and placed it on the counter out of casual reach. "We need his next bolt hole."

I looked at Viper, still stuck in her own thoughts. I snapped my fingers under her nose. She grabbed my hand, twisting to cause pain. "I have no more information. You must let me leave."

Andy looked to the officer at the door before saying, "You stay here. I am not letting anyone else get killed."

That would only be possible when Ivan Kuznetsov rotted in prison. "If he killed those men himself, he's covered in blood," I said. "He won't go far."

"He could have hired out the job," Andy said.

"I think he's getting too personal to trust anyone else," I said. I don't know where the feeling came from, but it felt right.

Andy called Gena. "What about the houses next door, any residents?"

She said something and then Andy ended the call. "They haven't checked yet. She'll call back."

"How long ago?" Viper asked. "How much time between the killing and the discovery?"

David pulled up a case file on his phone. "No time of death yet. The blood was still wet, so not long. You think he's cleaned up and gone already?"

Viper shrugged and reached for her bag. "I can't be sure what he's thinking. But the Wraith will advise him. If it was me, I'd tell him to clean up fast and find a place to hide for a couple of days."

A text buzzed on Andy's phone. "Bloody clothes and bathroom towels in the house to the west."

"You think he might lay low like Viper said?" I wanted to

believe we had breathing room. Time to find and follow a trail. My gut was rolling its eyes at my naiveté.

"I doubt it," David said. "We need to know why he decided these guys should be killed now. What he's planning to achieve."

My phone rang, Guy. I couldn't take it where anyone might overhear so I excused myself. The look on David and Andy's faces told me I wouldn't be keeping the contents of the call secret. The constable followed me to an empty office but waited outside in the hall.

"Yeah?"

"You saw the news?" No small talk, no attempt to get me to step away.

"The killings. Kuznetsov, we think."

"The guy's gone off the rails. You need to stay close to your friends with guns."

Like I didn't know that was the safest option. "I won't cower. He needs to be in prison."

I heard the sigh and waited for him to explain why I should leave him to the cops. "I figured you wouldn't do the smart thing. Look, I can get you a gun."

"I don't do guns. I wouldn't be able to shoot someone with one without hitting everything else in range."

"No problem, a pistol will do. Pretty much point and shoot."

If I said yes, he'd be in trouble with David for giving me a weapon, and his boss for helping me out. "No. I can handle myself. Do you know where he might be?"

"I don't discuss business, Charity," he said. "Even when it comes to a guy like Kuznetsov. We do better when we're low key. It means the cops occasionally arrest a few soldiers, but they can't take down the Angels as a whole."

"Kuznetsov isn't low key."

"Yeah, he's a fucking maniac. I mean he was bad enough before, but the Russians are always pushing the edge. This guy? Something happened in the last couple of days. He doesn't seem to care what the consequences are, like he doesn't plan to be here to deal with them."

If he was so far out of control, how did Kuznetsov hide so well? I knew I was taking a risk that Guy would cut me loose this time, but I had to ask. "Is he still doing business with the Angels?"

Guy didn't answer right away. I checked the screen of my phone to see if we'd been cut off. Nope. He was thinking.

"I know you can't share specifics," I said. "Yes or no would help. If he's still doing business, we might find him that way. If not, he might be on a suicide mission."

"Yes. There's only so many ways for us to get product. Until we find another supplier, we don't have a choice. We don't deal with him directly. He used to send the guy he killed this morning."

"Thanks. You be careful. If he killed your contact, he might come for you."

"We take care of ourselves." Guy told me to be safe and then ended the call.

46

When I rejoined the team in the break room, I came clean about the call. Well, more or less, as I didn't mention the offer of a gun. Mainly because I thought David might agree and make me take an official one, and someone would want to know who offered me a street gun. Guy was my contact, and I would protect him.

"If he's clearing the competition, there are a lot more gang leaders to take out." Andy was watching the TV report. It took a lot to fill a twenty-four-hour cycle, and they were making the most of the lack of information by using 'unconfirmed' and 'alleged' in every sentence.

I couldn't feel bad about hoping he was busy with that part of his plan for a long time. When he had the low-hanging fruit picked off, I became a priority.

"There's one loose end still free," I said. "Viktor's wife." I know it was a big assumption given what just happened to Alan and Dean, but I figured anyone in jail or under protection would not be in danger right now.

"We looked for her right after we pulled in Blackhouse and the Guptas," David said. "She's in the wind."

I told him about her aliases. "I tried to get her to turn herself in, but she had her own plans."

"She's not likely to come in now," Andy said. "We can look for her though."

I handed over the aliases. "My guess is she headed toward Kelowna or Kamloops for a flight out."

"You have a picture of her?" Andy asked. "Maybe facial recognition will catch her."

Did the smaller airports use the same technology as the international? Although maybe that's what he meant. Most of the flights from those two terminals would go to Vancouver, Calgary, or maybe Toronto. In two more days, she could be anywhere in the world.

I found the image from the adoption agency's website and sent him the link. "How much would she need to disguise herself to fool the facial recognition?"

"If she kept her face from the camera, that's all it would take." David looked over my shoulder at the image. "It's pretty hard to do that with all the cameras, but it is possible. If we get a potential hit, we can work backwards to gain recognition, maybe."

Viper kept suspiciously quiet during our conversation. I checked, and she was staring at the laptop with the crime scene photos. "You see anything?" I asked. "Something we wouldn't notice?"

She didn't take her eyes off the screen. "I'm trying to figure out who the Wraith copied for this. But I'm not having any luck."

"Does he have his own style?" She told us his style was to copy others, but maybe he didn't start that way.

"A long time ago, maybe, but I don't know what it is.

Look at this. The bedroom is a mess, but the bodies are nicely laid out. If that was all you found, wouldn't you think someone who cared about them, or some kind of serial killer, committed the murder?"

I pulled up a chair and a notebook, tuning out everyone but Viper.

The bodies looked like they'd been laid out, like for a viewing. "If not for all the blood. Would someone who cared for them be so overly violent?"

"Rage does things to people," Viper said. "But yes, serial killer is probably where the cops would go. So, they would be looking for similar murders."

I wrote that on my paper. Maybe I'd find a pattern here. Something pointing the cops on the wrong path. "If this task force wasn't in place, and this was just an everyday murder, yeah. I see how it would look. You think maybe this is a coincidence?"

It felt odd to be talking about catching a murderer with a professional killer.

"No," Viper said, "because of the other bodies. They would identify his men quickly. The tattoos say Russians."

"Okay. The body on the stairs?"

She frowned as if I'd come up with a hard question. "If you take out the blood? An accident."

"And the kitchen? That wasn't a simple accident or murder."

She looked at me with a smile. "No. But it looks like a *sicario*, yes? Punishment killing."

I sat back to think. I saw what Viper did, but why? "You think the Wraith didn't do this?"

She flicked through the pictures again. "A lot of rage here. We don't get emotional. If I left something like this at a killing, it would be because the client told me to. It is possible that Kuznetsov did this, but if it was the Wraith, he was acting on detailed instructions."

"Why?" Andy asked.

I hadn't even noticed them standing behind us. I was so focused on figuring out the message left for us.

"I don't care about why when I take a contract."

Motive was a strong tool for a case. I knew that from my own experience with regular clients as well as the few criminal investigations I'd been involved with. "I can guess. He's trying to stir up the competition. He's telling the local cartel operatives that he's coming for them. And he's telling his guys they better be loyal."

"Or he's telling us that we won't ever find him because he's unpredictable," Andy said.

"But he must still be in business," David said. "He can't get rid of all his competition because some are his suppliers or distributors."

"Sorry, it was no help," I said. "I hoped a theory would send us right to him."

David put his hand on my shoulder and gave me a gentle squeeze. "Not right to him, but you just came up with the plan. We go for his next business deal."

Viper gave a bark of a laugh. "Good. I did worry you would never come up with a way to stop him. You don't need me anymore, I'll be going."

"No. You need to stay here until we arrest him," Andy said. "If he sees you, he'll kill you."

"So? I live with that threat. Eventually someone will succeed in taking my place. I am very good at hiding."

Andy's phone buzzed. He checked the message. "Cynthia McCarthy thought the same thing. But we found her."

47

I t took about ten minutes for Andy to dispatch me and David to Cynthia's location. Me because she might talk if I'm there; David because, well I was on a list of people Kuznetsov wanted dead. I should be relieved they let me out at all. He said something about sending a few uniforms after us, but I didn't pay attention.

David drove to the Tsawwassen neighborhood where she'd bought a house under an alias: her mother's maiden name translated to English, and Viktor's mother's first name. Nadya Waters. There was definitely an advantage to working with people who had legitimate access to records.

The house was an A-frame with a small, landscaped garden in front. It sat on a side street with similar houses around the cul-de-sac. The kind of place that didn't see traffic beyond delivery trucks and commuter cars. No security cameras evident, but it was possible a canvas of the neighbors would find a few of those doorbell ones.

David told me to stay behind him as we approached the front door. He stood to the side and knocked. "Ms. Waters, police."

I pointed to the doorbell with the tiny lens. "She knows we're here."

He rang the bell and identified himself again.

"Maybe she's not home," I said. "I'll check around the side for a garage."

I moved before David could tell me to stick with him. The right-side driveway led to a carport. Yes, a silver BMW SUV sat there, maybe the same one that picked her up, but they all pretty much look the same. A door led from the carport to the house. The temptation to try it burned, but I held off. David needed to be the one going in first.

The hood was cold. The security light that came on when I approached clicked off. I checked for cameras and found none. That didn't mean they weren't tiny and well hidden.

I joined David at the front and reported what I found. I started to worry about what we'd find inside. "How did the cops find her?"

"Airport camera caught her face. Vancouver. She flew in from Kelowna, like you thought. But she had no outbound flight. Her plan was to make everyone think she left the country. Maybe she planned on going later. To be completely honest, this is a good place to hide out for a while."

"Not if the neighborhood is empty all day." My fear dissipated. Kuznetsov might find her, given time, but he wouldn't have access to the airport surveillance, so we might be ahead of him.

"Let's try the side." David walked away from the front door. "Will you stay at the corner of the building? I want to know if anyone tries to leave or comes near."

I positioned myself next to the down pipe. The only space not covered in plants. Some gardener made a mint on caring for this place. The quiet was getting to me. I mean, living in this peaceful place might be great, but as a stranger, I expected some Stepford robot was going to sashay down the street to make me conform.

"Charity."

David's call made me start. I pretended to be cool and strolled to the door. It was open. "Did you pick the lock?" He usually lectured me about doing that.

"It was unlocked when I got here. The vehicle too."

"Did you look inside?"

He shook his head. "I thought you'd like to join me before I went in. Get behind me again, just in case."

He pulled his weapon and held it in front of us, ready to shoot if necessary. The door led to a mudroom and then to the kitchen. Everything in sight was clean and sparely decorated. Cynthia either liked empty spaces or she hadn't taken the time to personalize her new home.

The living room and dining room were off the kitchen. Dining room in the back, living in the front. Both were devoid of life. A staircase went upstairs from the kitchen. I followed a step behind David. If Cynthia was in the shower, she might not have heard us enter; it might minimize the shock to see someone she recognized. If she wasn't home, we needed to clear the house before we settled in to wait.

Upstairs were three closed doors, one at the end and two facing each other. My gut was tight from waiting to encounter someone. Now we could be facing three some-ones, and Cynthia could be waiting with a gun aimed at whoever entered the room. David approached the first door on the right, holding a hand to tell me to stay.

He leaned against the wall and turned the handle, giving the door a little push. No murderous homeowner or assassin sprang out. We looked inside. A spare bedroom.

Decorated as if someone simply moved a showroom inside. The closet doors stood open, and the shelves and hangers empty.

The second door led to a decent-sized bathroom, also empty.

All we had left was the main bedroom and no side wall to speak of for either of us to hide behind. David motioned me back to the stairs, but I didn't budge.

He glared at me but reached for the door handle. Inside sat a king-sized bed and in the middle, on her back, lay Cynthia. A knife stuck out from her throat, blood staining the white covers.

48

Cynthia's murder caught me by surprise. I guess for some reason, despite evidence to the contrary, I'd believed her when she said she could take care of herself. She hadn't expected Kuznetsov to go on a rampage any more than we did. People in that state were unpredictable, but no less competent than usual.

David nudged me away from the door. I guess my DNA and stuff was already all over the house, contaminating the scene. He took pictures and sent them to Andy.

"Downstairs," he said when he finished. "We can wait in the kitchen."

Fine by me, far enough away from the body that I might be able to forget the details. Close enough to be in on the action.

I sat at the counter and waited for David to say something. Like I should have told them about Cynthia when I met her. She wouldn't be dead now if I got the cops or RCMP involved. Then I realized my little voice was undermining me. David didn't need to put a guilt trip on me because I was fully capable of doing it myself. I'd screwed up badly.

"It's not your fault," he said, sitting on the only other stool. "It's all over your face. You think you could have prevented this."

I wanted to accept his statement. Logically, he was right. I had offered her protection and she chose to run. I didn't kill her. "I know. I just can't help feeling like I could have done something."

He hugged me and I started to cry into his shoulder. He patted my back and let me sob.

When the whole embarrassing episode ended, he found some tissues and handed me a wad.

His phone rang. "Are you on the way?" The answer took no more than a few words and then David ended the call. "Gena and Luc are leaving the Richmond crime scene and should be here in ten. Andy will wait for us downtown."

"Is the other scene processed?" If Kuznetsov wanted to get away with all this violence, maybe keeping the cops hopping from one scene to another would work. If they couldn't process a murder properly, it would be harder to solve the case. I couldn't imagine a man bent on slaughter thinking that clearly.

"Andy sent another team there. He told me to stay in here. You can get a ride back to the office if you think it's too much for you to hang around."

Not a chance. As soon as I stepped back into the office, I'd be forced to fight if I wanted to leave again. "Maybe we can step outside for some fresh air."

I hopped off the stool and headed to the sliding doors leading to the backyard. The lawn was beautifully tended. Shrubs lined the edges of a fence. A pool at the back had a little fountain and a bird feeder. Hummingbirds squabbled about taking turns to sip some nectar.

I covered my hand with a tissue and opened the doors but stayed inside for a moment. It was so quiet outside I could hear the water burbling in the fountain. So different from my home. The harbor was always noisy. Even with no humans around, the seagulls screeched and the traffic a block away on Georgia rumbled.

"Are you coming?" I asked.

David put his phone on the counter and joined me, wrapping his arms around me and pulling me close. "I could live here," he said. "Imagine winding down after a day in this place."

"You'd need to wind down after facing the tunnel traffic every day." It might be peaceful here, but I wouldn't trade the bustle of my home for the hour or more commute.

I kicked off my shoes so I would get the full experience of the grass. It felt cool and damp on my soles. I turned to suggest David do the same thing.

A bullet whizzed past my head and dug into the fence with a thump. I dropped to the ground as David rushed to me.

"Are you hurt?" He had his hand on his weapon.

"No. Just surprised. Go."

He hesitated. I pulled out my phone. "Go see if you can catch whoever shot at me. I'll call Andy."

He still didn't move. I gave his leg a shove and he started running around the side of the house.

I pulled up my recent calls and hit Andy's name. While the line rang, I belly crawled inside the house before getting to my feet.

"Miller," Andy said.

I told him about the shot.

"Stay inside. Where's Anchor?"

"Looking for the shooter or some evidence."

"The locals will arrive before Gena. Let them secure the scene, and then you and Anchor come back here. No arguments."

I wasn't planning an argument. David stepped inside and closed the sliding door before pulling the curtains across. "Okay. Should we give our statements first?" I asked Andy.

"Make some notes. I don't want you hanging around at the scene." Andy swore at someone — not me, thank goodness. "Let me talk to Anchor."

I handed David my phone and went to grab his from the counter. I heard a siren approaching; we would be out of here soon. I couldn't go upstairs, but maybe I'd find something of use down here. Something that would point to how the killer knew she was here, or how they knew we were here.

"I hear them," David said. "We'll hand over the scene and leave."

I held up his phone for him to unlock and then wandered through the living room, taking pictures of things. I found a shopping list on a side table, and a printed receipt for delivery of a new TV right next to it.

The cops banged on the door and identified themselves. I opened it after peeking through the window to make sure they were not killers pretending. Then I let David take over while I made sure the images of the receipt and list were legible. Nothing else jumped out at me as a clue. The room was only dimly lit now that the curtains were drawn in the back, but turning on a light might destroy a fingerprint on the switch. So, I waited to be sent away.

49

A search of the area didn't turn up any killers, so David and I headed back to the office. I didn't say much on the drive, not because of shock or anger, both of which I felt, but because I was rehearsing my reasons for not being kept prisoner. I relied on them not 'protecting' David into custody, so if I was wrong and they locked him up, I had no way to avoid it. Not that I wanted him in danger; I desperately needed to be there at the end when they put Kuznetsov in cuffs.

"Why are you turning so much?" I asked. Since we left the highway, David had been zigzagging through the streets.

"Just want to be sure we're not followed," David said. "I know it's obvious we're heading back to the RCMP building, but if we have a tail, I'd like to identify the vehicle."

"You think he'll try again?" I didn't relish the idea of waiting to be killed for the rest of my life.

"We don't know if he, or she, meant to kill or only warn us. Professionals don't often miss."

I felt the rush of air as that bullet went past as if it just happened. "If I hadn't moved, I'd be dead."

David made the turn into the parking lot. A uniformed officer pointed us to the door. When we stopped, another man took David's key and told us to go inside. If someone was watching, they had no second chance to kill either of us.

"Are we sure there aren't drones?" I asked, remembering the call I received earlier. "If we can't come and go freely, we won't be able to stop Kuznetsov."

"Frequency jammer is taking care of any devices. It means we need to use landlines inside, and cell phones won't work in a two-block radius."

What about all the civilians? "How long can you keep that going? I mean, some of the people around here don't have landlines."

David looked at me like I'd said something stupid. Like I'd missed an obvious clue. I shook my head and shrugged. If I had, I needed to be told. My brain was occupied with the aftermath of the shooting and my plans to stay free from protection.

"The people who live around here don't own cell phones. They use a common landline in the lobby of their SRO. The only people in a two-block radius who won't be able to communicate are drug dealers and pimps."

Heat grew in my cheeks. I'd forgotten we were in the Downtown Eastside. I was so wrapped up in what I wanted that I'd ignored my surroundings. The RCMP were here because of the high crime rate. The people who lived here were so poor they lived in single room accommodations with no access to the things we took for granted. And that coffee shop? Why was it open when none of the people could afford what they sold? For the film shoot? Or were they a front for something? "Sorry. I should have thought."

The elevator door opened, and he gestured for me to go first. "You would normally notice. Don't minimize the impact of almost being shot on your ability to think things through."

We walked out of the elevator and followed an escort to the break room. Andy and Viper stood face to face, not quite yelling, but their body language suggested it wouldn't be long before things escalated to a full-on shouting match.

"You can't go out there," Andy said as I walked in. "He's targeted one of ours when he killed Phillipe. If he's that far along, he won't blink at killing you."

"You can't protect me," Viper said, her voice dropping to a whisper. "You had that guard under protection and he's dead."

"He wasn't under my protection," Andy said. "You are safe here. We all are. No one is entering or leaving until this is resolved."

Viper noticed me, or rather let us know she did. I figured she'd been aware of David and me from the moment we approached the room. She sat on a chair, not taking her attention from Andy. I could almost see her thoughts as she formulated and discarded escape plans.

"She's right," I said. It was selfish of me, but if they managed to keep Viper inside, I had no chance. "And you admitted she's not under arrest."

Andy deflated, but he wasn't ready to give up his plan to save her life. "Why are you so determined to put your life in danger?" he asked her.

I understood his concern, and his frustration. She was a killer and he still cared for her safety. I don't think he'd come to like or respect her, far from it. If he could come up with a legitimate way to arrest her, she'd be in a cell. But he knew better than to pull the protected witness status game. The same as arrest, but you didn't need to commit a crime.

Having two women determined to take risks regardless of his wishes must be pushing all his buttons.

Viper looked at the screen now that the media had found the two new murder sites. "That," she said, nodding toward the screen. "I have experience in protecting myself. You won't do what is needed if Kuznetsov comes at you."

"He already has," I said. I was supposed to be taking her side to make my own case, but I couldn't. No matter what she thought, we were safer here. "Someone shot at me."

My words didn't change anything. "See. He can't protect you."

"She's alive," David said.

Viper stood and started gathering her belongings. "Not by anything you did. If the Wraith is taking orders from Kuznetsov, he missed because his orders were to miss. I'm leaving now. I've been a target before. I can protect myself." She picked up her cell phone and swore because there was no service. "I need to make arrangements."

"I give up," Andy said. "I have a vicious mob boss to catch. You can use a landline to make your arrangements. We'll give you an escort to get you as far as you need."

"Your lines are probably not secure." Viper stuffed her phone in a pocket. "I'll take the escort. We'll go somewhere public, and I'll call for transport." She looked around the room and then sat. "How long will this take?"

50

I n the end, Andy managed to delay Viper's exit by two hours. A pair of officers went along as her escort. Andy checked their body cams and their weapons personally. Everything was in working order. When it came time for her to go, Viper walked in the middle of these two imposing guards. They left the building the same way we entered, from the front door directly to a vehicle.

"Where are they dropping her?" I asked. I hadn't been part of the preparation plan. David had insisted I talk to a counselor while we had time. The session was long enough for me to say I was fine, break down and cry, confirm I was fine and then admit I wasn't but didn't want to stop until Kuznetsov wore handcuffs. The counselor seemed satisfied with my progress.

"She wouldn't tell me," Andy said. "We'll get it from the body cam when she tells them."

The speaker remained silent for now, but we saw Viper on both sides of a split screen with camera one and two identified in the lower left corner of each stream.

"Everything is fine," Viper said. "Look, no one has approached us. No car is tailing us."

"We're outside the jammer range," camera one said. "Could be a drone."

"Okay. I won't argue about this. You can drop me off at this address." She handed a piece of paper to camera one. Andy noted the address and sent a team to check it out. "You'll let me out in the alley behind the house. You'll drive away."

I wondered what she would do when she realized there were cops already on site. And if she was even going into the house. Maybe it was a safe drop off, and she'd walk to the real location. "Do we have drones?" I asked.

"Unfortunately, we need a warrant to use one," David said.

The address was a twenty-minute drive away. Viper stopped talking after giving the instructions. None of us wanted to leave, but watching a woman staring out a tinted window was a sure-fire way to doze off.

"Gena and Luc are finishing up with the Tsawwassen scene," Andy said. "Going back to the Richmond one now."

"What happens if there's another killing?" I asked. "I mean, Gena and Luc can only handle so many, right? Is there another team ready?"

"I talked to my sergeant," David said. "She'll make a detective available if we need it."

"I'm hoping we get Kuznetsov before things go any further." Andy switched his attention back to his phone.

"We're at the location."

The words dragged my attention back to the screen. Everything looked the same. With the tinted windows, you couldn't be sure if the vehicle was parked or in motion.

"Then I'll be going," Viper said. She waved at the camera and undid her seatbelt.

"We'll escort you inside," camera two's owner said. "Our job is to get you here safely. Until you are inside, you aren't safe."

I watched Viper open her mouth to tell them no, but she stopped before words came out. Her shoulders dropped and she forced a smile on her face. "To the door and not inside."

"We don't need to come inside," camera one said. "But you go in before we leave. Or is this just a decoy?"

"No. This is where I get what I need to leave," Viper said. "Fine. To the back door. Are you ready?"

Seatbelts released and the view became jerky as the officers exited the car. The split screen changed to one view of Viper's back and the other of a back fence, then an untended yard with a small house at the end. Gray pebble dash exterior, wooden back stairs and faded blue back door.

"You can stay down here," Viper said.

I assumed she didn't want them crowding her on the small landing in front of the door.

"We come up with you," camera one said.

She turned to look right in the camera lens and stared at us. "I didn't agree to this. Are you sure you want to piss off someone who knows how to get away with..."

Smart enough not to say murder on camera, she just grinned.

"Either we go with you, or you get back in the vehicle." Camera one officer was getting tired of this game. "You can do that voluntarily or we can cuff you. Maybe tase you to make it easier."

"I am not committing a crime by telling you to leave," she said. This time her tone was cold. The game was over for her.

"You are a person of interest," camera two said. "We can take you into custody. If you don't cooperate, we can charge you with resisting."

That seemed over the top. I looked at Andy to see a grin on his face. He shook his head and turned back to the drama on the screen.

"Fine. It's going to be crowded, and my contact won't be happy to see you there."

"Too bad," camera one said. "If we don't go inside, you have nothing to complain about."

She swore. I didn't speak the language she used, but no one could miss the vitriol in the tone. "You can follow me," she said.

I don't know if it was on purpose to create some shock and awe kind of vibe, or just an old set of stairs, but it sounded like storm troopers running up the steps.

"We leave when you're inside," camera one reminded her.

We watched as she retrieved a key from a lock box and pulled open the door.

The screen went black.

"Explosion. Send fire and ambulance," the driver said. Suddenly the screen showed images again. Flames and debris all over the back of the house and yard.

I heard David telling a dispatcher where to send the emergency services, but I couldn't turn away from the view. The driver shifted to point his body cam at the entire scene. Someone's arm stuck out from under the burning door. Another body lay buried under the staircase that had come free of the house. I couldn't see evidence of the third body, the one that would be smaller, Viper.

51

The room was silent in the aftermath of what we just witnessed. I couldn't pull my thoughts together. I didn't trust Viper, but she shouldn't have died that way. And the two officers with her. Why did they insist on escorting her to the door? They could be alive now, inspecting the damage and working the case.

"The fire and ambulance will be there soon. The secondary team we sent are stuck in a major traffic accident. I've recalled them," David said. "I think you should stay away from this particular investigation, Andy."

Andy turned away from the screen slowly. He blinked at us and then straightened as he pushed the shock to the back of his mind. I recognized that look. A professional got used to dealing with the present in the present. All the emotional turmoil got stuffed in the back and if they didn't deal with it, then it became fuel for drugs, alcohol, or gambling. Whatever helped them quiet the pain for a while.

"Yes. VPD needs to take this one. Can you make sure the lines are open to us?" He looked at the screen again before turning it off. "We need to get the bastard now. No one is safe out there. I'll call Gena and Luc back in. We can't lose anyone else."

"You think Kuznetsov targeted the officers, too?" I asked. If he was going for police targets, he was definitely out of his mind. Now everyone in or out of uniform would be on the hunt.

"He didn't protect them," Andy said. "He didn't care who was with Viper. And this Wraith guy is just as out of control, or he would have done the kill differently."

While Andy contacted Gena to tell her what happened, I started a fresh pot of coffee. It was already late in the day. We'd been working on catching Kuznetsov for more than a week. Andy was right. This had to end, if not today, then by tomorrow. We couldn't take months to tangle him up in minor charges. We couldn't take the risk that his bosses would make more of a mess cleaning up after him. And if he killed the local gang leaders, it left others wanting revenge, and a big gap in the power structure. We'd be eyeballs deep in cartel within the week.

We needed a plan. "Viper said he needs to leave someone standing. He doesn't have the supply and distribution networks to be the only player, right?"

"We don't know who he'll keep," David said. "It's only a guess about wiping out the competition. He's only targeted the Fallen Lotus so far."

I knew exactly who I'd leave standing if I was Kuznetsov. Someone with almost a global reach. Someone with the connections to keep distribution running. "We need to get him in person. If he's going to a business partner, he might not expect a trap. Or he might think they've been cowed by the murders."

"If we knew his next location, I would have people there to take him," Andy said. "There are at least five gangs he could work with who were grateful for the killings, or too scared to go against him."

"Not all of them," David said. "You have undercover operations running? We do too. It's worth a try."

That would take too long, getting permission, contacting the operative, setting up a deal. And it could all go wrong in the end, anyway.

"Or we can reach out to the head of a gang." I didn't want to come out and tell them my plan. If it was David's idea, or Andy's, maybe no one would resist or think it too risky. "You know who runs the local gangs. One of them must want to get Kuznetsov as much as we do."

David got up and poured our coffees. He put the mugs down absently, his mind on something other than refreshments. I hoped his thought focused on the name of a gang boss we could use. I'd prefer not to burn a contact, but I would if it meant getting Ivan Kuznetsov locked up in a tiny cell.

David glanced at me, then Andy. He took a long swallow of his coffee and put the mug down. "We don't go in to kill him, right?"

"Take him off the streets," Andy said. "Not kill him. He doesn't deserve an easy way out."

"What about self-defense?" I asked. "If he tries to kill us? One of you can take the shot, right?"

Andy rubbed his eyes before answering. "Yes. Our job is to protect, so anytime someone tries to kill in our presence, we do what it takes. But it's too soon to talk about that. We need to pick the ally in this, and I want people who aren't torn up about what's happened. That part is going to be hard."

"I trust you and David to be clear on the objective when

we make a deal," I said. "I don't carry a gun, so I won't be a problem."

"You won't be there," Andy said. "Too much chance Kuznetsov will use you to escape or provoke violence."

It was the completely wrong time to say I refused to step back. I planned to be in the room, not as a target or a potential victim. I wanted to see Kuznetsov go down. When we got the trap solidified, I planned to play a key role and there was nothing either David or Andy could do about it.

"Who do we approach?" Andy asked. "We can't trust any of them. But if the deal is right, we should be okay for one shot."

"What kind of deal?" I'd give a free pass on something to get Kuznetsov, but the official line wouldn't be that clean.

"They'll want some charges dropped on one of their guys, or immunity for some past crimes." Andy checked his phone. "They'll ask for information on undercover ops, or something like that, but it's just bargaining. You were right. They want him gone as much as we do."

"We'll need to get the parameters in place before we call," David said. "The Crown will have lines they won't cross."

"Will they want us to look the other way while they kill him? The gang I mean, not the Crown Counsel." If a hit was out on Kuznetsov, it would complicate things.

"We'll tell the gang leader not to get in the way," David said. "As part of the deal."

"No one will put a hit on him," Andy said. "If the hit fails, the backlash wouldn't be worth it. Maybe if his bosses wanted him gone it would be different. I don't think they would put out a contract. They'd send someone he trusted — one of his own guys if possible. I'll see if the Crown will talk now."

52

I waited until Andy was busy with the Crown to talk to David. In the aftermath of the explosion, I had an overwhelming need to confess everything I'd kept from him. If I was going to die, I didn't want to leave anything hanging.

"I think I need to come clean about something," I said. Clumsy, but between the ticking clock on Kuznetsov, and my rising fear that I was next, I had no time for finesse.

"Yes." David put down his phone and gave me his whole attention. "I know you've been hiding stuff from us. I trusted you not to take too big a risk. But we can't go ahead with this unless we're all sure we can rely on our knowledge of the game."

"Thanks for making me sound like I knew what I was doing," I said.

"You do know what you're doing. So, what are you hiding?"

We were alone in the room. Andy might walk in any minute, or anyone on the team, and I couldn't tell them without David on my side.

"Not a lot," I said. "Frankly, I've forgotten what I told you and what I kept to myself, so you might know this already."

David nodded encouragement and took my hands. He waited for me to spill everything.

I told him about all the calls I'd received warning me off. I told him about seeing Popov at the movie set. If his lawyer was there, Kuznetsov might be in deep with the production. A tidy way to launder money since movies and TV swallowed funding and had very creative accounting to keep the profits from actors and producers with percentage deals.

"Okay. Good to know," David said. "It doesn't change anything."

"No, but I have an idea and I don't think you'll like it." I'd been thinking about how to put this since the talk about offering a deal to a gang leader. I'd been successful in making it their idea, but now I needed to tell them who we should approach. David knew that I had a way of getting to one.

Gena walked in and saw us. She tipped her head in question and I said, "Give us a minute." I wanted privacy, but not for long. I could trust Gena to keep the rest of the team outside.

"What idea?" David asked. "And do you think telling me first will give you an ally?"

"Think is a strong word; hope is more like it."

"Until I know what you think, I can't make promises."

I couldn't delay any longer. "I have a contact in the Angels."

"Yes, I didn't go looking for who it was because that's your business until it becomes mine."

"This contact might be willing to put us in touch with the local chapter leader."

"We can get to him if you can't. You think the Angels might be a safe bet?"

Why I couldn't just get the whole idea out in one breath was beyond me. "No one is a safe bet. I think going through my contact might make things easier. I know the Angels aren't happy with the current situation. We need them to set up a meeting with Kuznetsov and then take him down."

David let go of my hands and clasped his between his knees. Looking down, he thought it over. I loved his ability to detach from the immediate emotions and look at the whole picture most of the time. I couldn't rush him, and since getting Guy to answer or return my text could take time, there wasn't much I could do. A few minutes here might save us hours of hashing out the problems.

He got up and opened the door. "Come on in."

I'd lost him as an ally. He would have told me if he was on my side. Now Andy joined Gena as she sat at the table.

"Charity has an idea," David said. "I'm not a hundred percent on-side since it puts her in danger, but Andy, it's your call. She's come up with a pretty good idea."

He let me explain, and I kept it to the facts of the plan and tried not to fall into the trap of convincing them about any detail. Or demanding to be part of the take-down. It wasn't the time, and it would only get in the way.

"Why do you think the boss will agree?" Gena asked.

"The deal is good. And I may be totally off base, but the Angels are the only gang who collects toys for kids," I said, not sure if that was enough reason. "They maintain a connection to the community beyond crime."

"You think Kuznetsov might be keeping them as the single partner?" Gena asked.

I'm not sure why Andy wasn't questioning my plan, but maybe he was just waiting to shoot me down when Gena finished. "They are global, right? Or mostly. It would make sense. And they don't have a reputation for the kind of violence other gangs perpetrate. No drive-by shootings that take out innocent bystanders. No mass slaughter."

"They've learned the benefit of putting business before revenge," Andy said, finally joining the conversation. "Make no mistake, they are a violent criminal organization. Charity, I think going in through your contact is a good idea. I will not put you at risk. Gena can be our insider for the meeting. Good plan, Charity."

What the hell? I almost yelled at him that it was my plan, and I wouldn't be cut out, but a more rational voice in my head said to take a breath. And that breath gave me an answer that sounded logical. "It will depend on what my contact says and what his boss wants. I'll talk to him, and if he's okay with me giving you his identity, I'll pass it along."

None of that could be interpreted as a 'yes, of course I'll stand down.'

"Contact him," Andy said. "Just ask for a meeting. The less he knows in advance the better."

I sent the text. *RCMP and cops want to set a trap for our Russian friend need your help.*

53

I put my phone in my pocket after sending the text. I didn't want anyone to accidentally see the contents. I might be a rebel, but I didn't want to be caught and put on a time out.

"How long does he usually take to respond?" Andy asked.

"Depends on how busy he is or if he's pissed at me," I said. "But it won't be long. What did you get from the Crown?"

"We have a deal to offer," Andy said. "I'm not telling you the details, and I plan to give as little as possible."

Without the details, I couldn't be the one negotiating. "And if I'm the only one he'll talk to?"

Andy raised an eyebrow that I took to mean, I'd better not make that happen. "I'll give you the information you need, but I would prefer to do the talking."

"While we're waiting, we need to run down the callers. From those threats," David said. "All of them, not just the ones we've already checked."

No way was I giving them my phone. Andy ordered the

jammer turned off after Viper and the two officers died. To be honest, I think it inconvenienced the cops more than any spies. "If I give you the numbers, would that be enough?"

Gena held out her hand. "Not the numbers, just let me transfer some data from your phone and you can have it back."

And if Guy called while she was doing it, we'd be screwed. "Not until we've talked to my contact."

"You could give us access to the records with your provider," Andy said.

Out of the corner of my eye I saw David start to chuckle.

"No. When I've set up the meeting, you can look at the specific calls on my phone while I watch."

Andy's face hardened. Hearing no from a team member came as a surprise, I guess. I put my hand in my pocket and held my phone. It buzzed. I pulled it out and looked at the screen. "This is him. I need privacy."

I answered the phone with, "Hang on for a sec." Then stared at them to make my point.

No one argued or stalled. I was alone in seconds.

"Okay, we're alone," I said. "What do you think?"

"You are far too smart to do something this risky," Guy said. "Why would we help?"

I told him there was a deal on the table and I'd get the details when he said yes. "Provisionally, of course, until we've got something agreed. I don't expect you to trust me enough to guarantee cooperation."

"The boss is interested, but you need to be ready fast."

"He doesn't want anything?" I couldn't believe that it would be that easy.

"He'll want everything he can get," Guy said. "We're meeting with Kuznetsov tomorrow night. Charity, you need to pull your shit together. No promises. That deal has to be platinum level."

"So, your boss knows about me?" I always thought Guy was going behind the gang's back to talk to me. If the boss knew about it, we might both be on borrowed time.

"Always has. He's okay as long and I don't share chapter business, but this might be the end of our relationship. Are you okay paying that price?"

I didn't want to pay any price, but if finding another contact to replace Guy, not necessarily another Angel, was the cost of getting a killer off the streets, I'd pay it. I usually didn't need information about criminal activities anyway, and I didn't plan on making a habit of chasing gangsters. "If I have to," I said. "So how do we do this?"

"The boss will call on this number in two hours. You need to know the details of the deal and be able to negotiate. If he likes what you have to say, you're in. If not, we won't talk again."

"Why is Kuznetsov meeting with you?" I had a guess, but if I knew the answer it would help with the plan.

"He says it's to make a new partnership. We think he's coming to take us out like he did with the Fallen Lotus guys. We're preparing to defend ourselves."

"When he calls, I'll be with an RCMP officer and a cop. That needs to be okay, Guy. I won't step outside this building to talk. I need them with me for the negotiation."

"Yeah, I'll tell him. They don't get to talk. And, Charity, you don't tell them my name, right?"

"I promise."

I ended the call, checked my battery power and decided to charge my phone just in case. I opened the door expecting to see three people waiting to come back in and found just the one officer guarding the door. "Can you let them know to come back?"

He gave one nod and said, "Deacon is finished," into the air.

I went back in and checked the time. Late, too late for coffee if I hoped to get any sleep. In two hours, it would be tomorrow. Within a day it would be over one way or another.

I told them what happened when David and Andy came back.

"Good. No need for anyone to be bait," Andy said. "When we know the location, we can surround the place as soon as Kuznetsov goes inside."

"I wouldn't plan on it being that easy," I said. "Wait until we talk to the boss before we make plans."

"Just putting it out to the universe," Andy said with a chuckle. "Yeah, we'll need someone inside. Gena might still be the best for that. A woman gets dismissed as no threat when all the alpha males are around."

"Shouldn't she be here when we talk if that's the case?" I knew she'd obey orders, but she should get a say in the plan.

"She's preparing the team to investigate the bombing," Andy said. "She'll join us soon. She still needs to check your phone, Charity."

I thought about the people who loved the officers who died in the blast. I'd gotten so wrapped up in the end goal that I'd pushed the latest killings to the back of my mind. "Did someone notify the families?"

"We hire counselors to do that," Andy said. "It's hard enough to lose an officer, let alone tell the family."

54

Two hours felt like days. We had nothing to do. Too little time to bother napping, and the sun would be up soon, making it too light to sleep. All we needed to do to catch Kuznetsov was negotiate with the head of the local Angels chapter. The killings were being investigated somewhere else in the building, and no one wanted our help.

Eventually, we sat in Andy's office, circled around his desk with my phone in the middle, waiting for it to ring.

"You don't agree to anything without my say so," Andy said. "You know the parameters of the deal. We don't want to go to the maximum if we don't have to."

Like I never bartered before. I nodded and kept my focus on the phone.

"And no agreeing to dangerous plans," David said. "He'll try to get all the advantage on his side."

If he thought I'd sit out the final stage of this case, he didn't know me. It wasn't up to me what I did during the meeting. Guy's boss would have his own ideas about who participated. Really, it was all up to the boss. If he didn't agree, we had no other next step. I wouldn't be able to get a location for the meeting from Guy, or the time. We didn't know Kuznetsov's location, so we couldn't follow him. Good or bad, the Angels were in control.

The phone buzzed and I hit accept.

"Who's in the room?" a deep kind of raspy voice said.

I introduced David and Andy. "They won't talk."

"Fine. Guy tells me you want to come to our meet."

How much did he know about our relationship? I had to assume everything. "We think we can get Kuznetsov if you agree."

"And what do you think the Russians will do to us when they find out we set the trap?"

I hadn't thought about any repercussions for the gang. I was only focusing on getting this particular Russian off the streets. Intellectually, I knew someone would replace Kuznetsov, but I guess deep down I thought they would be grateful to us. "We can do it so it looks like we scooped you too. Maybe take in a couple of the members?"

"So, I sacrifice a couple of the people I'm supposed to protect?"

He had me tied up in answering detail questions before we agreed on a deal. If I answered him, we wouldn't move on. "We can figure that out. Look, Kuznetsov is coming to your meeting regardless of what you do with us. We have a deal to make it work for you. We need you to agree before we talk the little stuff out."

I couldn't believe how calm I sounded. This was dangerous work, and my voice came out steady, my mind focused, almost like I knew what I was doing. Then I looked down and saw my fingers clasped around each other while my hands shook. I couldn't relax them or my shoulders, which seemed to be trying to wrap themselves around me like armor.

"Look, we don't know why he's coming. If it's to make a deal, we do business. If he's out to kill us? Well, we have plenty of ways to win a fight without involving the cops."

If he didn't want to work out a plan, why had he called back? I tried to straighten in my seat and relax my hands because the tension was starting to build in my chest. Hard to keep your voice calm when you couldn't breathe.

"Maybe that's what the Fallen Lotus guys thought," I said. "And it's what Viper thought." I stopped because listing all the people who died made me feel a little sick. "What makes the Angels different?"

He chuckled, like I'd been particularly bright with my question. "We won't be alone. And if this is business, cops will get hurt, federal or local, it won't matter."

"What if it wasn't cops?" I kept my eyes on the phone screen, but I couldn't miss the reaction from my partners. I didn't mean only me, but if the objection was about the cops in the room, then they could be outside. "If they stayed outside until someone gave a signal?"

"You want us to call for help like we can't handle a situation?"

It seemed he needed me to spell it out, but first I wanted him to agree to a deal. "Look, we're back in the details again. What will it take to bring you on board with any kind of plan for us to take him down?"

There was a long pause. I didn't for a second think he was pondering the question. He would have his bottom line thought out before making the call. I let him play his games for now.

He broke the silence. "Okay. No charges for anything

that happens at the meeting. Any current outstanding charges get dropped. We get a free pass for a month."

I pressed my lips together to stop my immediate response. I took a few seconds to pretend I needed to think about it. Then I said, "I need to confer. I'll mute at this end for a few minutes." I hit mute. It gave me a chance to ask for Andy's input. At the other end, I heard a few swear words and then silence. The call was still active, which I took as a good sign.

"Only one of those things is okay," Andy said. "No free pass for a month, all current outstanding charges stand. Anything less than murder gets a pass for the duration of the meeting."

That seemed fair to me, but I knew the boss would want to win. I hit mute again. "Are you ready?"

"Get on with it, princess."

"You can forget the free pass. I can't drop any current charges. But anything that happens at the meeting other than federal crimes is okay."

"You are the only person in the meeting with us," the boss said, all business now we were haggling. "You turn a blind eye to anything that we do. You take him down outside the meeting."

"I won't turn a blind eye to murder," I said. Most of the other crimes I wouldn't ignore didn't happen at a meeting. "We can't guarantee the takedown goes on outside. If he's there to wipe you out, it will be too late for you. We'll make it look like a raid if we come in. I'll have a way to signal the cops."

David grabbed my wrist to get my attention. I shook my head and didn't turn away from the phone as I pulled my wrist free. We didn't have time to argue.

"We won't murder anyone where you'll be a witness.

We'll let you have a signal. And I'm sure your two cops will be happy for me to say we'll keep you safe."

He ended the call.

"You should have told him no," David said. "Does he know what you look like?"

"I think so, but my contact does." I didn't mention Stick because I hoped he wouldn't be there. I guess I hoped Guy would make sure he didn't come to the meeting and screw everything up. "I don't think we can fool him."

"Gena can go in for you," Andy said, ignoring my last statement.

"No. It's too much of a risk to send her."

"Not as much a risk as sending you," David said. "You think you can deal with it, but you have no idea how fast things can go very wrong."

Why are we arguing about this? "I agreed it would be me. He said they would keep me safe. I'm going."

Andy and David exchanged glances. I hoped they weren't sharing some cop signal to arrest me. If I started arguing with them now, it would get ugly. But I was ready to do it.

"I don't like it." Andy shook his head. "I can't help but think you set us up."

"You get your way," David said. I heard the warning in his tone that I better survive.

"Thanks," I said. It was better to be gracious and not smug. "I need a disguise, right? I mean, something to stop Kuznetsov identifying me right away."

A text arrived from Guy before either could answer. The time and place of the meeting. In fourteen hours, we would be done with this case. The meeting was at an address in East Vancouver.

55

The address belonged to a long-closed restaurant. The windows were boarded up so no one would see in. When we stepped inside, I saw the interior was cleared out. The electricity still on, so we didn't need to wait in the dark, but no chairs or tables, and nothing on the shelves behind the bar. Cobwebs decorated the corners with strands hanging from the ceiling. From the dust coating them, the spiders were long gone.

The neighborhood was as run down as our location. I noticed a few buildings with flickering lights inside, possibly squatters, but most were dark and likely in the same state as the restaurant. Before long, some developer would tear this building down and replace it with a concrete tower.

Andy and David waited outside with a team of heavily armed RCMP constables.

My signal was in my right earring. I pressed the stone and a beep, or something would sound in Andy's ear. I had two signals. One press meant come in ready to take Kuznetsov down — and a couple of gang members for show. Two presses meant emergency, help, come in guns blazing.

Whatever signal I sent, when I reached to my earring, the Angels would scatter.

I was in as Guy's girlfriend. I needed to be able to move quickly, so no hooker stilettos; I had on cowboy boots and tight jeans along with a cropped tee shirt and leather jacket. Since Kuznetsov had seen me in the nightclub, I had on a short pink wig and very dramatic makeup. At a quick glance I should pass as not-Charity. If he recognized me too soon, we were in trouble.

I went in with Guy to find the boss inside. A big bear of a man with a graying beard and wild hair. No one else waited for us.

"The others will be here in five minutes," Guy said. "We need to make sure you understand what's going to happen. You do everything I tell you. No arguing. We said we'll keep you safe, and that's how it will go."

The boss kept silent. I guess he was sizing me up.

"No argument on that. I don't have a death wish. But I need to send the signal, right?"

"Yeah, that's the plan."

"Okay. When is Kuznetsov getting here?"

"A while," the boss said. "One more condition."

Fuck! I wasn't expecting him to renegotiate at the last minute. "What?"

"You and Guy are done," he said. "I was okay with him giving you tips because you never asked about our business. But you're done when this is done."

The menace in his voice was hard to ignore. This wasn't up for negotiation; he was issuing an order. "Will Guy be okay?"

"Not planning to kill him or kick him out," the boss said.

"Fine. I'll find another contact somewhere." I turned to Guy. "I'll miss you."

"I won't miss your nagging," he said. The squeeze he gave my shoulders put a different meaning on his words. He'd miss me too.

The back door scraped open, and Angels started filing in. It turned out to be only eight in total, two other women hung on the arms of the first men to enter. Not the whole chapter like I'd been imagining for some reason. Since a few of these were going to end up in jail today, I guessed this was some kind of punishment or a way of proving their loyalty.

The last person to walk in the door made my heart stop. Stick. The guy who thought Guy should share me with him.

"What's she doing here?" Stick demanded as soon as he saw me. So much for my disguise, but unlike Kuznetsov, he'd talked to me and gotten in my face. And I'd been in drug-addicted hooker mode at the time.

"Love makes us stupid," Guy said, pulling me closer and kissing me.

"No fucking kidding. Let me know when it's my turn." Stick stepped closer and loomed over me.

"Stand down," the boss said.

Stick immediately stepped back and moved to the shadows.

"She's off limits," the boss said. "You all know the plan."

The plan we'd sketched out an hour ago was that the cops would clear the streets of any stray gangsters or drug dealers. The working girls would be warned to stay off the streets until the shit went down. The Angels who waited outside were for getaway purposes only, so if it came down to a gunfight, no one would complicate matters. Whatever happened, Kuznetsov was going to jail tonight. And it would all happen inside the building to minimize the risk to bystanders.

"You know who's taking a hit to keep us clear," the boss

said. "We'll get you out, that's part of the deal, but a day or two in jail is in the cards."

"Yeah, a little vacation," one of the Angels said. "We got something worked out to make it look legit."

I wanted to ask so many questions, but I knew to keep my mouth shut. This was their territory. My job was to call the cops inside and maybe act as a witness if I had to go to court.

"Everyone carrying?" the boss asked. "Just in case."

At his question, every man in the place held up a handgun, some of them two, and one guy had managed to hide an automatic rifle somewhere.

The boss looked at me. "You go behind the bar if shit goes down."

I nodded. I wouldn't argue with orders if things went sideways. I didn't mention that the bar couldn't protect me against bullets.

"We reinforced it," Guy said, then quietly so that no one else, in particular Stick, could hear, he continued, "You go behind and duck below the metal plates. Stay down until your boyfriend comes to take you out."

We stationed ourselves at the side of the wooden bar. All I needed to do was crouch down and take two steps to the corner.

I heard a phone buzz and wished I held mine, but I'd agreed to come in with no devices. I guess they didn't want me recording anything.

"He's on his way," Stick said, reading a text. "Five minutes."

I didn't know what to do. I should be preparing somehow. Like putting on armor and checking my weapon was loaded with one in the chamber. But all I could do was wait the longest five minutes in my life.

56

Kuznetsov didn't come alone. I didn't expect him to. Even for legitimate business he would have protection. First to enter was a henchman. The tall, blond, high cheekbones, Adonis look destroyed by the dead gray eyes. Behind him came Ivan Kuznetsov. Balding, solid and just plain mean looking. He was high on something. His fingers twitched constantly, and he kept looking over his shoulder.

The last to enter was a man who could only be the Wraith. Thin, like he's come to the end stage of a terminal illness. Hair dyed black, clothes black, gaze constantly roaming the room for threats.

I moved closer to Guy. I didn't mean to do it, but something inside me pushed my body toward protection.

All three men carried guns. Weapons in holsters for now, at least the ones I noticed. Any of them might have knives tucked away, or a garrote or a Taser — or another gun.

Stop listing weapons.

I'd been in shitty situations before. I'd been threatened

with death and torture more than once. This time, no threats, but I had no confidence that I could talk my way out. I wished I hadn't agreed to the one-way signal. I should be wired and able to sub-vocalize my report. If that wasn't a thing, it should be.

"You came here to talk," the boss said. "Let's get started."

"What? You going on a date later?" the henchman said. "You aren't in control here."

The boss just gave a slow blink and kept his eyes on Kuznetsov. "I only deal with the man in charge. I thought that was still you, Ivan."

First name basis? Is this a trap? I must have tensed because Guy gave my shoulder a squeeze. I remembered I trusted him and why. They would want a bigger catch than me. I forced myself to relax and listen. I would need to report on everything, and fear did shitty things to memory.

Kuznetsov had been staring at the boss the entire time I went from panic to not-quite-relaxed. His eyes were the only still thing about him. Whatever he'd taken had him making constant tiny movements, fingers tapping on his leg, shoulders twitching, foot tapping.

"You came here high to do business?" the boss finally asked, breaking the silence.

"I do business however I want." Kuznetsov's voice was deep and muddy, like the words formed in the back of his throat. "You know what is happening to your competition?"

The boss nodded. "A bit too public for my taste."

"Sends a message." Kuznetsov turned his gaze on the room. "Not a lot of your bikers here."

He wanted to know where the others were. Was he expecting an ambush?

"This is all I need. You here for a chat? We could be drinking somewhere if we're not doing business."

"Small talk," Kuznetsov said. "You like small talk, yes?"

It didn't feel like small talk to me. It felt like delaying. He was waiting for something. My brain started running images of every stupid action movie I'd ever seen. The cops lying in pools of blood. Russian mobsters surrounding the building with AK-47s pointed toward us. Our only hope a single hero beaten but not out. That's where my imagination collapsed. Even in panic mode, I couldn't see Guy, the boss, or Stick coming up with a catchphrase and saving the day.

"If you're here to fuck around, we got better things to do." The boss shifted his weight like he was getting ready to leave. "Call us when you're ready to do business."

The other Angels changed position and I thought the plan was blown. Then I noticed the movement put the women close to the bar. I wouldn't be alone back there if this went sideways.

The Wraith leaned in to say something to Kuznetsov.

"Not yet." Kuznetsov said, flicking his fingers to signal the man to move back.

"Ivan, let's get this going, then we can have a shot of vodka and all go somewhere with chairs and booze." The boss signaled to Stick, who put a bottle of *Pulgar* and two shot glasses on the counter.

"Let's drink first." Kuznetsov took a step toward the bar.

Stick moved to block access to the bottle.

"I'm tired of playing your fucking games," the boss said. "Look, we're here for business, or maybe you think you can take us out like the Fallen Lotus assholes. If you're here for business, weapons on the bar and stand back. If it's a fight, we're ready."

Every Angel and the two women pulled out guns. Guy handed me a pistol.

"I don't know how to use it," I said, pushing it toward him.

"Point and shoot. It's ready to go. Only if you have to." He shoved the gun in my hands and nudged me toward the end of the bar.

I admit it was better to be armed in a room where everyone else felt free to brandish their guns. I really didn't want this to escalate to a fight, but Guy was right. As a last option.

I reached for my ear, but Guy tapped my arm down. "Not yet."

"Are you going to keep your weapons?" The henchman asked.

The boss smiled and pointed to the bar. "We aren't the ones slaughtering the competition. We keep ours. We promise to stay cool if you're here for a deal."

The two women slipped behind the bar and put their hands out for Kuznetsov's guns. The Wraith stepped closer to Kuznetsov.

"You want us to trust you? Why?" Ivan asked.

The boss kept his attention on Kuznetsov and answered, "Like I said. We're not interested in being the only player. Too much work. And anyone trying to take the whole pie is going to live a short life."

Kuznetsov stared back for a moment, then laughed like it was all a big joke between friends. He nodded to the henchman and the Wraith to follow orders.

"Yours too," the boss said.

Kuznetsov shrugged and pulled out a big silver handgun from a shoulder holster and handed it to his henchman to surrender. "So now you feel safe?"

57

I don't know about the Angels, but I didn't feel any safer now that Kuznetsov and his people pretended to be unarmed. I would only feel that when David walked in the door and all the bad guys wore cuffs and all the weapons confiscated, because I'd just come to the realization that I didn't understand this world enough to be sure who to trust. Even Guy might be ready to betray me. I tried not to puke or look like I needed to.

Guy had a firm grip on me so I couldn't go hide. He leaned in close and whispered, "If you move now, they'll notice you. When I let go of you, you signal the cavalry and duck behind with the other girls."

My entire being wanted to run and duck, but I stood still as an answer. The Angels had relaxed around me. Weapons still out but now pointed at the floor. Stick glanced my way and frowned. I ignored him. Guy's hold relaxed but didn't move. I had to believe the boss knew what he was doing, and I wasn't here to be sacrificed along with these Angels.

"Never safe around you, Ivan. What's with all the drama

out there? I mean, I get the killings; we don't want too much competition. But bombs?"

Kuznetsov gave a little smile like he was suppressing pride. "Quiet work doesn't make headlines. I send messages my way."

"That kind of message brings the wrong attention," the boss said.

Kuznetsov's smile turned into a snarl. "I don't answer to you. I do what is necessary. You just hide in the shadows."

The boss didn't respond to the obvious challenge. Kuznetsov was looking for a reason to fight. I couldn't say what his henchman would do, but the Wraith guy would probably be happy to start another slaughter. He'd moved to blend with the shadows in the corner. He was fooling no one. The boss concentrated on Kuznetsov, but the rest of the Angels kept an eye on the other two men.

Adrenalin burned through my veins, making me hyper alert. The henchman was like ice. Everything about him tightly in control. No twitches in his fingers, no shifting of his weight. He watched Kuznetsov, probably for orders. I had no doubt he would act on even the slightest signal.

The Wraith was different. He scanned the room, paying little attention to Kuznetsov. His right hand kept feeling his pocket and returning to his side. He had some weapon in there, but it would be small. A remote detonator? He wouldn't set off a bomb when he was inside the building unless I was right about his terminal illness and he didn't care so much about getting out of here alive, but he kept very close to the exit. And a grenade would be small enough to fit in his pocket.

I turned my gaze to the Angels watching the killer. One of them stepped to block the exit. I wasn't the only one thinking this was a trap.

"What business are we doing tonight?" The boss gestured to the bottle on the bar top. "We've got a fine vodka, so I hope you have something worthy of it."

"We are here to tell you the new deal." Kuznetsov stepped toward the boss. The Angels lifted their weapons again. "You think they can stop me before I kill you?"

"Maybe not. Why don't we just talk business and drop the threats. There's ten Angels across Canada waiting to take my place. I go, the Angels continue. What happens if you get killed?"

Kuznetsov smiled again and my gut tightened. He was completely unstable. "I don't plan to die tonight. Yes, let's talk business, and then we drink."

I tried to lift my hand to signal, but Guy tightened his grip again. "Not yet."

I had no choice. Turning to tell him I didn't think it would be a good idea to wait until the bullets whizzed over his head would draw attention. I was safe here if I stayed quiet. I imagined David standing outside the door with a gun pointed at whoever walked out, ready to rush in at my signal.

The boss appeared to accept the smile as a good sign. "So, you want us to take on the Fallen Lotus slice of Vancouver?"

"You think you can handle them when they find out?" Kuznetsov asked. Whatever he'd taken was wearing off. His body had stopped all the twitching, but now his skin was dull, and his words came out slower. "They also have people waiting to take over the top spot."

This discussion wasn't clear enough to be useful in court. Now that they were dancing around the business talk, I had time to think beyond hiding behind the bar. The two women still stood there, so maybe I was the only one who thought we teetered on the edge of war. Everyone else in the room had experience in this type of situation. I didn't have some special insight to let me ignore all the menace in the air.

"So, it wasn't about competition?" the boss asked. "You just didn't like those particular guys?"

"You could say that," Kuznetsov said. "I also needed to clear house. I respect loyalty. I left two messages at that house." He turned away and looked straight at the Wraith. "I don't suffer incompetence either."

"Loyalty is important," the boss said. "So, what's the business? More volume? New products?"

Kuznetsov smiled again, and the image of a snake ready to strike hit me. He was playing with us. He enjoyed this game.

"New products," he said. "You could say that. I lost my supplier. I need to replace him. So new business to you, I think, but not to me."

"What is it?" the boss asked. He was not enjoying the game. I trusted that he knew how to handle it, but he must be getting ready to bring things to a head one way or another.

"Kids. I need a supply for various purposes."

The Angels tensed. I knew this was a line they drew. No kids. Not for trafficking, or dealing, or anything.

"No."

The boss didn't move, but I felt the mood change in the room. The Wraith, no longer calm, stood poised like a predator. The other Angels were aiming now, not just pointing their weapons in a general direction. The only person who didn't react was the henchman.

Guy let go of my arm.

58

For a second, I didn't know what to do. Guy gave me a shove and my mind engaged. I ducked and slipped behind the bar where my two companions were already sitting calmly, waiting with the vodka and glasses on the floor beside them.

"Smart move," I said, nodding to the bottle.

"The boss would kill us if we let that fucking Russian asshole put a bullet in this," the woman nearest me said.

I know I should be hitting my signal, but the situation was stuck somewhere between come on in and *get in here as fast as you can*. If I pressed once, I might be setting off a gunfight, and I didn't get the feeling we'd reached the level of an emergency yet. I could still hear the conversation, but not seeing the body language made a huge difference in my stress level.

"I'm Charity," I said.

The blond woman pointed to her chest. "Rosie, and that's Belle. You with Guy?"

So, Rosie and Belle didn't know about my part of the

plan. "For now," I said. It was the truth, and he could explain what went wrong when we apparently split up.

We settled against the back cupboards and waited, guns in hand. I stared at the metal plates behind the bar. They didn't look new, so this place must have some history.

"You do the business I tell you to," Kuznetsov shouted. "No one denies me."

"We don't do kids," the boss said, voice quiet. He wasn't playing any games now. "If that's what you came for, go somewhere else. Plenty of people out there who don't draw the line."

"The last person who said no to me is in little pieces in the morgue."

"I got no problem putting you down, Ivan."

"Maybe your men don't want to die."

Now I wanted desperately to see what was going on. If Kuznetsov had a mole in the Angels, we would all die because I didn't send the signal to Andy.

"Sure," the boss said. "Any of you want to work with this asshole?"

There were a lot of murmured rejections. I didn't hear anyone making a move.

"Ilya, bring the ladies out," Kuznetsov said.

Rosie stood at the words and pulled Belle with her. She looked down at me. "Better than getting dragged out."

I noticed they both moved their gun hands behind them. I did the same before reaching up and pressing my signal twice.

"You I know," Kuznetsov said, staring at me. "Bring her here."

Clearly my disguise was not effective. "I'm happy here," I said. *Where is the cavalry?*

Ilya, the henchman, grabbed my arm and pulled. I tightened my hold on the gun and let him drag me toward Kuznetsov.

"You have people waiting to save you, yes?" Kuznetsov said. "They are... busy."

I heard the back door scrape. "Not that busy," I said.

"Kill them!" Kuznetsov screamed as he grabbed me and held me like a shield.

I heard one shot behind me. Kuznetsov spun me around to see the Wraith on the floor, blood oozing from his head. When we turned back, the bikers were slipping away and letting the RCMP in.

"I said kill them!" Kuznetsov screamed again.

Ilya held up his hands and let his handgun hang from his middle finger. Then he lowered himself to the floor, pushed the gun away, and waited.

Kuznetsov's hands eased their grip on me. I took the opportunity to adjust my own gun. He wrapped one arm around my neck, his other extended forward with a match to the big shiny gun he'd put on the bar. "You let me go, she lives."

No one lowered a weapon or even moved. David stood beside Andy. Both of them had rifles aimed at us. I knew they wouldn't be able to hit Kuznetsov without going through me. I couldn't just drop to the ground like I'd done before because he held me too tight.

"Let her go and no one needs to die." Andy lowered his weapon but no one else followed. "Just let us take you in. You call your lawyer, and we talk."

Kuznetsov shook now, not in anger or fear, but in jerky spasms. He was hurting for another dose of whatever he'd taken earlier. He held the gun steady despite what I felt from his body. My gun was at my side now. He might not know I have it. Or if he noticed, he didn't think I had the guts to shoot. He might be right.

"You can't keep me here," Kuznetsov said. "When I get away, she dies first. When I finish the woman, I kill that coward." He nodded toward Ilya. "Then I come for each of you."

I couldn't talk with his arm holding me so close. I stared at David and then down at the gun in my hand. He gave a tiny nod. Did that mean I should shoot? What if I missed? Fuck, this was not worth it.

"You bring a lot of attention to the business," David said. "How does that go down at home?"

The arm tightened, and I had difficulty breathing. "Reputation. No one betrays us. No one says no to us."

"Just lower your weapon," Andy said. "No more bodies. Your pet hitman is dead. We didn't kill him. You can't be sure the next bullet isn't headed for you. You're alone against all these men."

"You won't let me kill her," Kuznetsov said. "Too much paperwork for a civilian, yes?"

Did he really think everyone thought like him? He didn't care about the repercussions if his behavior in the last couple of days was an example of how he worked. The threat of paperwork wouldn't stop David, or Andy, or any of the other cops doing the right thing.

We were in a shitty position because of me; I should have signaled sooner. It wasn't going to get any better unless I did something to stop it.

I glared at David, turned my wrist inward and pulled the trigger.

Kuznetsov went down, his arm releasing me to grab at this wound. His gun skittered across the floor. Every armed

RCMP officer rushed us and shoved the barrels of their weapons in his face.

David pulled me away from the action. "Are you hurt? Why did you wait so long to signal us?"

I started laughing and couldn't stop.

59

I 'd spent the rest of the night in my own bed with David curled around me. It seemed like years since I'd last been at home, but it was only a couple of days. When we woke, David made me call the RCMP counselor and make an appointment to deal with what happened. I didn't argue with the logic; the last thing I wanted was after-effects of almost being killed to get in the way of any jobs.

Now we waited in Michel Benoit's office to debrief. Andy, David, and I sat on one side of his small conference table, Michel on the other. He didn't look happy to see me — too bad.

"You should have called in the team when you hid," Michel said. "Your friend in the Hells Angels knew it was time. Why did you wait?"

I had the same question. What was I thinking? But no way would I let Benoit know. He'd been against my partici-pation the entire case. And how did he know about Guy? "At that point there was still a possibility that Kuznetsov planned to do business. Nothing illegal had happened, and I didn't want to set off a war in that room because I called you in too soon." It actually sounded like a good plan now. Maybe my mind works well under pressure.

He turned from me to Andy. "You did not instruct her sufficiently? How was she unsure?"

"The situation was fluid. I trusted her to know what to do. It was successful. No one but an assassin died. We got our target and his second in command. One of them will talk."

"And the involvement of the Vancouver Police Department? You felt that was a success?"

Is this guy always looking for a problem?

"Yes," Andy said.

Benoit pushed his chair away from the table, stood and returned to his desk. "I expect a full and detailed report on my desk today."

We were dismissed. We moved to Andy's office. I wanted more details too. Not an official report that would stand up in court. I wanted the story.

Andy sat and motioned for us to do the same. "You'll need to write out your version of the events," he said to me. "David can help you get it in shape."

"Fine," I said. "Look, this was a success, right? He seemed to be pissed off."

"He always seems that way," Andy said. "Yes, we succeeded."

"So, what happens now?" I asked.

"My secondment will end as soon as the paperwork is done," David said. "If Kuznetsov isn't smart enough to make a deal, we'll go to court. Make sure you keep lots of notes."

"Sure. And did I do a lot of damage to him?"

"Broken leg, but he'll survive." Andy turned on his computer monitor and read something. "Did you mean to kill him?"

"No. But I wasn't really in a position to choose where the bullet went. I'm very happy to go back to jobs that don't require guns."

David took my hand like he was going to give me bad news. "He's not going anywhere. His gang is quiet and will be until the new boss arrives. Probably in a day or two. It won't be the same."

"The new kind of kingpin is different," Andy said. "More businesslike, less kill the competition. The violence isn't good for their bottom line. You'll be safe from retribution. The Angels might have a bit of explaining, but no one is going to take them out."

It would be a while before I felt truly safe. Hearing the words and believing them were two different things. The Angels didn't need help taking care of themselves. I would miss Guy, but like I'd told the boss, I could find someone to take his place. He wasn't the only contact I had with the darker parts of the city.

"So, I'm done. I'll send an invoice," I said. "Thanks for letting me play on your team. I never want to do that again. Back to insurance fraud, estates, and wandering spouses for me."

"You get a few favors too," Andy said. "Be careful. Remember this all started because Glenda Blackhouse thought her husband was up to something."

True, my cases sometimes went from humdrum to what the fuck is happening without warning. Good to know I had a few favors piled up from the RCMP.

He dismissed us and I followed David to a computer station to start writing up my notes. "Thanks for not yelling at me about waiting," I said to David.

"You were there. Don't let anyone undermine you. No

one, not even your contact, knew the right time to call us. I trust you."

"Who killed the Wraith?" The question had been niggling at me all morning. If not the rescue team, which of the Angels?

"No one knows," David said, turning to me. "It wasn't us or the Angels. The henchman was on the floor and Kuznetsov had you, so they couldn't be the shooter."

"What do you think happened?" I could make a guess, one of the girls behind the bar with me, or maybe one of the Angels, or even the henchman. Too many possibilities to be sure.

"A contract, but on the Wraith," David said. "I think Kuznetsov was only responsible for some of the murders. I think the Wraith overstepped. So, a contract to take him out from a family member, or someone from the Fallen Lotus gang."

"Or from Russia." I hoped it meant we had a respite from insane murder sprees.

WANT MORE?

Are the murder sprees over? Use the QR code to pick up your copy of Conviction and join Charity as she battles to save an innocent woman from life in prison.

~

If you enjoyed reading Wrath, please consider helping other readers to find the story by leaving a review.

FREE EBOOK

Claim your copy of Buying Into Death when you use the QR code to sign up for my newsletter and follow Charity as she solves her fastest case yet!

ALSO BY P A WILSON

For more books by P A Wilson

Use the QR code below or go to pawilson.ca

ABOUT THE AUTHOR

Perry Wilson is a Canadian author based in Vancouver, BC who has big ideas and an itch to tell stories. Having spent some time on university, a career, and life in general, she returned to writing in 2008 and hasn't looked back since (well, maybe a little, but only while parallel parking).

She is a member of the Vancouver Writers Social Group, The Royal City Literary Arts Society, and The Surrey Writing Workshop. Perry has self-published several novels. She writes the Madeline Journeys, a fantasy series about a high-powered lawyer who finds herself trapped in a magical world, the Quinn Larson Quests, which follows the adventures of a wizard named Quinn who must contend with volatile fae in the heart of Vancouver, and the Charity Deacon Investigations, a mystery thriller series about a private eye who tends to fall into serious trouble with her cases, and The Riverton Romances, a series based in a small town in Oregon, one of her favorite states. Her stand-alone novels are Breaking the Bonds, Closing the Circle, and The Dragon at The Edge of The Map.

For more information
www.pawilson.ca
pawilson@pawilson.ca

ACKNOWLEDGMENTS

People think that the process of writing is solitary. That's not the case for me. I have help from so many people it would be hard to acknowledge everyone, but I'll give it a try.

The support and inspiration I get from my writer's groups is incalculable. The Vancouver Writers Social Group opens my mind to other ways of telling a story. The Royal City Literary Arts Society gives me the opportunity to meet and share with other writers who have more knowledge than I do. The Other 11 Months group is where I learn about getting the words on the page. And my critique group who helps me find the best parts of the story I want to tell. Thanks to all of the members of these great groups.

Last of all, but definitely a huge part of the process, my beta readers. These are the people who love stories and are willing, and more than able, to tell me if my finished story is ready for you, my readers.